D1189458

MY HEART LAID BARE,
by CHARLES BAUDELAIRE

Charles Baudelaire was born in Paris in 1821. His passionate and almost unnatural love for his young widowed mother was shattered when she married General Aupick in 1828. He came to see Aupick as a symbol of the respectability and authority he loathed, and his loss of the love of his mother as a symbol of his destiny in the world. His parents opposed his determination to become a poet and embarked him for India but Baudelaire left the ship at Reunion and returned to Paris. He set up an apartment on the Ile Saint-Louis, which he furnished in decadent style, filling it with gilt and damasks and paintings by Delacroix. Here he set out to embody his ideal of the Dandy. He contracted dangerous debts and his life of desperate excess soon became depraved and sordid when he began the disastrous liasion with the mulatto actress Jeanne Duval, the *Venus Noire* of his poems. In 1857 he published *Les Fleurs du Mal*. He was prosecuted and fined for offences to public morals and a ban was imposed on the more obscene poems in the work which was not lifted until 1949. By 1864, Baudelaire's resources were exhausted and he fled to Brussels where his ruined constitution finally gave way. He was brought back to Paris in 1866 suffering from general paralysis and lingered on until 31 August 1867, when he died.

A characteristic theme of Baudelaire's is "l'horreur et l'extase de la vie." He found inspiration in the streets and the mysterious hidden life of Paris, and also in the spirit of evil itself. A sense of damnation provoked him to blasphemy; *"Enfer ou Ciel, qu'importe?"* he wrote. Beauty, to him, already contained the elements of its own corruption. *My Heart Laid Bare* and the other prose works published in this volume exhibit all Baudelaire's characteristic themes and are written with a disturbing blend of intellectual precision and romantic beauty, and with a sarcasm which merges into squalid decadence.

CHARLES BAUDELAIRE

MY HEART LAID BARE AND OTHER PROSE WRITINGS

TRANSLATED BY NORMAN CAMERON
Edited with an Introduction by Peter Quennell

PUBLISHED BY THE SOHO BOOK COMPANY
1 BREWER STREET LONDON W1

MCMLXXXVI

Published by
THE SOHO BOOK COMPANY
1/3 Brewer Street, London W1R 3FN
1986
Mon Coeur Mis a Nu
First published in this translation in 1950
© Weidenfeld and Nicolson Ltd, 1986

British Library Cataloguing in Publication Data

Baudelaire, Charles
    My heart laid bare and other prose writings
    I. Title   II. Quennell, Peter
    III. Mon coeur mis a nu. *English*
    844'.8   PQ2191.A22

ISBN 0-948166-07-X

Note on the translator: John Norman Cameron (1905–1953), poet and translator, was educated in Edinburgh and at Oriel College, Oxford. He worked as an Educational Officer in Southern Nigeria until the Second World War. After the war he joined the J. Walter Thompson advertising agency. His Collected Poems, edited by Alan Hodge, were published by The Hogarth Press in 1967.

Publisher's note: The opinions expressed herein are those of the author and not of the publisher.

Printed and bound in Great Britain
by Redwood Burn Ltd, Trowbridge, Wiltshire

Cover design, title page and introductory material
© The Soho Book Company 1986
Designed by Sally McKay at Graham Rawle Designs

CONTENTS

INTRODUCTION

In the record of every literary critic, even the keenest and most open-minded, there are sins of omission that he can never wholly live down: a moment when he has failed to pay homage at the shrine of Unknown Beauty: when obscure genius has passed unrecognised: worse still, when unwillingly and uneasily conscious of the claims of a talent he cannot fully understand, he has dismissed it with the help of a few evasive sentences. Such was the procedure adopted by Sainte-Beuve, appraising the poems of Charles Baudelaire. The poet's mother was an old friend; and the critic had followed the young man's early progress with somewhat apprehensive interest. Then, during the summer of 1857, *Les Fleurs du Mal* had received the attention of an Imperial censor: he had been haled before a correctional court: certain poems had been condemned as obscene, and the writer and his publisher had been fined and reprimanded.

Despite this initial reverse, Baudelaire, four years later, elected to stand as candidate for the Académie Française. It was a desperate and ill-judged move. What place on the official Olympus could be found for so rebellious an artist, so unconventional a human being, whose verses were little read outside a small admiring coterie, and who, passionately as he longed to succeed, both for his mother's and for his own sake, could scarcely bring himself to pay the customary round of ceremonial visits? Alfred de Vigny gave him generous encouragement: Lamartine was "amiable": but

Sainte-Beuve prudently held back, seeking a formula that would not unduly compromise him. He discovered it at length; and, enumerating the candidates for Olympus in his *Causerie de Lundi* of January 20th, 1862, he described Baudelaire as the architect of ingenious poetic "follies", as the inhabitant of a *"singulier kiosque faite en marqueterie d'une originalité concerteé et composite attirant les regards, à la pointe extrême du Kamtchatka romantique . . . . . ."* There he sat, smoking his hubble-bubble, a capricious but gifted and (Sainte-Beuve hastened to add) an entirely harmless solitary. He was by no means the *loup-garou* his adversaries pretended:

> "What is certain is that M. Baudelaire improves on acquaintance; that where one expected to find a strange and eccentric personage, one meets a polite, deferential and exemplary candidate, a pleasant young man, well-spoken and altogether conventional in his approach."

The faint praise of a troubled elder critic has seldom been more damning; and not for the critic alone, but for many readers of a subsequent period, Sainte-Beuve provided a means of escape from the problems of the poet's genius: he could be written off as a perverse experimentalist, unconnected with the main tradition of French poetic literature. Nor were his advocates more happily inspired. Enthusiasts of the later 19th century, particularly in England, tended to emphasise a single aspect of his protean temperament, to depict him as an amateur of esoteric vices and dark unlawful passions. In the second series of *Poems and Ballads*, Swinburne, whose literary likes and dislikes were always furiously one-sided, crowned the misconception with *Ave atque Vale*, a magnificent piece of elegiac word-spinning:

> For always thee the fervid languid glories
> Allured of heavier suns in mightier skies;
> Thine ears knew all the wandering watery sighs

Where the sea sobs round Lesbian promontories,
The barren kiss of piteous wave to wave
That knows not where is that Leucadian grave
Which hides too deep the supreme head of song. . .
Thou sawest, in thine old singing season, brother,
Secrets and sorrows unbeheld of us:
Fierce loves, and lovely leaf-buds poisonous,
Bare to thy subtler eye, but for none other
Blowing by night in some unbreathed-in clime;
The hidden harvest of luxurious time,
Sin without shape, and pleasure without speech;
And where strange dreams in a tumultuous sleep
Make the shut eyes of stricken spirits weep. . . . .

Indeed, in England at least, only during the last generation
have we begun to appreciate the full scope of Baudelaire's
poetic mastery. At times he was apt to parody himself;
in youth, the aristocratic pleasure of displeasing was one
he had much cultivated; and, to the end of his life, when
confronted by the spectacle of bourgeois complacency and
humbug, it amused him to retaliate with an explosive
paradox. Baudelaire sometimes wrote "in the manner of
Baudelaire"; but today this element of self-parody and the
streak of sensationalism, which a modern French critic has
called his "*satanisme a bon marché*", seem less and less
significant, just as we have learned to discount his occasional
vulgarities of expression—for example, those "*divans
profonds comme des tombeaux*", over which the late George
Moore used to hold up pale, plump hands in fastidious
disapproval. Than *Les Fleurs du Mal*—a title, by the way,
which was not of Baudelaire's choosing—few collections of
verse published during the Industrial Age have continued
to exert a more decisive influence: certainly there is none to
which we return more often, which preserves a greater air
of freshness and offers more surprises at each successive
exploration. Baudelaire's finest verse combines the delicacy

and subtlety of French with something of the brazen sonority
of the mightiest Latin poets. It incorporated the harmonies
of the past; and, as Jules Laforgue once pointed out, it
added a new and poignant note to the orchestra of modern
poetry—*"le miaulement, le miaulement nocturne, singulier,
langoureux, désespéré, exaspéré, infiniment solitaire"* of a
poetic intelligence lost in the huge industrial labyrinth.
Yet, as Laforgue goes on to observe, how courageously he
accepted some majestic commonplace, how boldly he would
employ some apparently humdrum phrase!

"After all the daring flights of romantic literature, he was
the first to introduce those matter-of-fact comparisons which
in the harmonious flow of a period suddenly bring one down
to earth".

And Laforgue thereupon proceeds to applaud:

"that uncompromising nobility which enriches his
interesting, captivating vulgarisms; a way of writing—
without any attempt at prudish, banal periphrasis—
that self-confidence of the great martyr which makes it
possible for him to produce such lines as:
    Les persiennes abris des secrètes luxures,
and a page later,
    Andromaque, je pense à vous"

The present introduction is not primarily concerned with
Baudelaire as a poet, but rather with the prose-extension of
his poetic faculties. Among modern prose-writers he stands
in the front rank; for he believed that the poetic gift was an
attitude towards life, and that a poet worthy of the name
must necessarily be a critic, both a critic of literature and a
critic of society: all great poets, he declared, became naturally
and inevitably critics; he pitied those poets who were
guided solely by instinct and regarded them as incomplete.
The poet must be a self-conscious craftsman, an intellectual
artist. He must seek the laws that govern his own activities,
and must attempt to systematise the enjoyment that he

derives from the activities of others. *"Je résolus"*, he explains at the beginning of his essay on Wagner, *"de m'informer du pourquoi, et de transformer ma volupté en connaissance."* Thus, in addition to *Les Fleurs du Mal*, he left behind him an assemblage of critical essays, unusually solid and well-argued yet lit up by constant flashes of imaginative insight. Like every critic, he was sometimes misguided; but, unlike *"l'oncle Beuve"*, in his appreciation of his contemporaries he was never ungenerous or luke-warm. Obviously, his cult of Poe was excessive, his championship of Wagner partisan. Not all the painters he admired have kept their interest today. We prefer to remember Fromentin's books: Baudelaire's description of a Boudin sunset has more literary charm than the original canvas (one suspects) may have possessed aesthetic value: he found a good word for Meissonier, and was occasionally tolerant of the work of Ary Scheffer. Yet, when the reckoning is finally calculated, he emerges with a formidable credit-balance of brilliant observations, which reveal not only his feeling for art and his knowledge of the artist's task, but his profound understanding of the social world about him.

The critical essays were not his sole achievement. Besides the essay dedicated to Constantin Guys, *Le Peintre de la Vie Moderne* ('The Painter of Modern Life'), in which he embroiders his critical theme with superbly imaginative hardihood, this selection includes a splendid sheaf of prose-poems, the private journals that he wrote at the end of his life, and a fascinating disquisition on the use and the abuse of drugs. Such a selection is admittedly incomplete. It represents, nevertheless, both the flexibility of Baudelaire's style and the diversity of his interests. It serves to show how faithfully and closely, throughout an existence that apparently went on from disaster to disaster, storm following storm, with rarely a quiet interval, he continued to pursue the path of literary self-perfection, undeterred either by public reverses or by the long series of private misfortunes that had harassed him since early youth.

Baudelaire's view of the artist's function is inseparably linked to his theory of the Dandy. But before attempting any general description of his aesthetic standpoint, it may be as well to touch briefly on the various works presented here. Among the earliest are certain of the *Petits Poèmes en Prose* ('Short poems in prose'), a project with which he was concerned between the years 1855 and 1863. What he intended to do he explains in a prefatory note:

"It was when going through, for at least the twentieth time, the famous *Gaspard de la Nuit*, of Aloysius Bertrand, that the idea came to me of attempting something similar and, in descriptions of modern life, of applying the technique that he had used in depicting the life of the past. . . . . Which of us, in his ambitious moments, has not dreamt of achieving the miracle of a poetic prose, musical without rhythm or rhyme, strong and supple enough to adapt itself to the lyrical impulses of the soul, to the undulations of reverie, to the stirrings of the consciousness. It is, above all, from frequenting enormous cities, and from observing the complexity of their innumerable inward relationships, that this obsessive idea is born."

But he confesses that, once having started work, he had discovered that his project was developing along entirely unexpected lines. Bertrand had merely provided a hint: Baudelaire's prose divagations remain essentially Baudelairean, a reflection of the same intelligence and an expression of the same sensibility that crystallised in *Les Fleurs du Mal*. We see the same clash between real and imaginary worlds: the propensity to dream and a hankering to escape from life—"*n'importe où hors du monde*" into some fabulous " *pays de Cocagne, ou tout est beau, riche, tranquille, honnête; où le luxe a plaisir à se mirer dans l'ordre. . . . d'où le désordre la turbulence et l'imprévu sont exclus"*—are again counterbalanced by a puritanical devotion to the task that he had set himself. *A Une Heure du Matin* ('One a.m.') concludes with a prayer:

> "And do you, O Lord my God, give me grace to produce a few lines of good poetry, so that I may prove to myself that I am not the most abject of men, that I am not inferior to those whom I despise".

—while *L'Invitation au Voyage*, ('Invitation to the Voyage'), one of the most nostalgic of the prose-poems, ends with an attack on dreaming:

> "Dreams, forever dreams! The more ambitious and delicate the soul, the more its dreams are impossible of realisation. Every man carries within himself his own dose of natural opium. . . . and from our birth to our death, how many hours can we count that have been filled with active joy, with planned and successful purpose?"

Rimbaud was to describe Baudelaire as the prince of *voyants* and first of visionary poets; but his visions were derived from his contemplation of the actual world, and his reveries centred around some concrete object. Although he was interested in drugs, and in the distortion and perversion of the senses which drug-addiction favours, his experiments had a very definite aim—he had hoped, not to deaden and curtail, but to heighten and enlarge, his awareness of the surrounding universe; while the title that he gave to his book is an indication of the disappointment that later overwhelmed him. There was no substitute for the life of deliberate effort, no relief from the exhausting vocation of poet, critic and observer! The first essay of *Les Paradis Artificiels* ('The Poem of Hashish'), appeared in September, 1858, some fourteen months after the publication of *Les Fleurs du Mal. The Painter of Modern Life*, which was shelved for two years before it found an editor, finally

reached the public in the winter months of 1863; and during
the spring of the following year, the poet, his health failing,
at the end of his resources, accepted voluntary exile. Alone
in Belgium, a country he detested, he wrote *My Heart laid
Bare*, a sketch for the "terrible book" he did not live to
finish. Were it ever to appear in completed shape, he
announced when he was writing it, the autobiography of
Jean-Jacques Rousseau would seem insipid by comparison!

Little of Baudelaire's prose was undistinguished; but
nowhere does his natural distinction emerge with greater
clarity than in his long imaginative tribute to the genius of
Constantin Guys. The poet and draughtsman were close
associates. Side by side in the gas-lit streets of Paris, among
its theatres, cafés and brothels, its pleasure-gardens and
parade-grounds, they had studied the spectacle of urban
civilisation from a hundred different points of view—in the
alleys of the Bois de Boulogne, through which superb
carriages, every one a triumph of the coachmaker's art,
whirled their resplendent human cargo—

> ". . . . down an avenue, zebra-striped with light and
> shade . . . . . a bevy of beauties, reclining indolently,
> as if in a cockle-shell. . . . . , idly bathe in the breeze
> of the drive"

—in the resorts of the fashionable *demi-monde*, irradiated by
the presence of young and lustrous courtesans—

> " . . . . the *femme galante*, in the flower of her beauty,
> aspiring to the airs of a patrician, proud both of her
> youth and of her luxury, into which latter she puts all
> her gifts and all her soul. Delicately, she turns up,
> between two fingers, a broad panel of the satin, silk
> or velvet that floats around her, ... and thrusts
> forward a pointed foot. . . . ."

—and in the squalid factories of commercial pleasure,
haunts of the lowest and most unsuccessful prostitutes—

> " . . . . heavy, gloomy, stupid, garish, their eyes

glazed by brandy and their foreheads bulging with
petulance"

who, nevertheless, as they strutted or sprawled or lolled
among their brutish clientèle, "in the indolent stupors of
café existence . . . . sprawling on divans, with skirts
tucked up before and behind in a double fan, or balanced on
stools or chairs", achieved, now and then, an air of savage
elegance:

> "Sometimes they unintentionally fall into attitudes
> of an audacity and nobility that would enchant the most
> sensitive sculptor—if only the sculptor of today had the
> courage and intelligence to find nobility everywhere,
> even in the mire. . . . ."

The Painter of Modern Life is a panorama of Parisian
miseries and splendours: it is also a condensation of
Baudelaire's theories on the relationship of art and life.
Turn, for example, to the third section. Genius, he declares,
has much in common with the state of early childhood:

> "For the child everything is *new:* he is always
> *exhilarated*. Nothing more closely resembles what is
> called inspiration than the joy of a child absorbing form
> and colour. . . . . The nerves of the man of genius
> are strong; those of a child are weak. In the former,
> reason plays a considerable role; in the latter almost
> the whole being is occupied by sensibility. Nevertheless,
> genius is simply *childhood rediscovered* by an act of will;
> childhood now endowed, for its self-expression, with the
> organs of a man and that analytical power which enables
> a man to put order into the automatically amassed sum
> of physical experiences".

For the artist is never merely passive and receptive, a
tremulous sea-anemone opening its tentacles towards the
nourishment with which chance provides it. No, the true
artist is keenly selective, rigorously critical, and to child-
like impressionability joins an adult understanding. He is a

man of the world in the highest sense of the term, ". . . . a man of the world as a whole, a man who understands the world and the mysterious yet legitimate reasons for all its habits". He takes a passionate interest in the manifestations of the contemporary spirit: "His business is to separate from contemporary fashion whatever it may contain of poetry within history; to extract the eternal from the ephemeral". But, although a zealous observer of the modern world, he is not its dupe or victim; and to this extent the artist resembles the dandy, another type of self-constituted rebel and self-ennobled aristocrat, in revolt against the pattern that vulgar commercial civilisation is always seeking to impose on him, a representative of "the best element in human pride—-that need, which nowadays is too uncommon, to combat and destroy triviality."

It is in Baudelaire's eleventh section, however, entitled *Eloge du Maquillage* ('In Praise of Cosmetics'), that we reach one of the most characteristic statements of his aesthetic doctrine. The majority of errors relative to beauty, he announces in his second paragraph, are derived from the spurious moralisings of eighteenth century philosophers. Rousseau and his contemporaries had exalted Nature as the source of beauty, truth and virtue. Baudelaire draws the exactly opposite conclusion: "Everything beautiful and noble is the result of reason and thought. . . . Evil arises of itself, *naturally* and by predestination; good is always the product of a creative skill". Hence the poet's intense admiration for what, in a noteworthy passage, he calls *"la majesté superlative des formes artificielles"*: hence his preference for those landscapes from which organic nature has been excluded— *"un paysage fait avec la lumière et le minéral, et le liquide pour les réfléchir!"* In this, as in much else, Baudelaire, it must be admitted, was often inconsistent. Virtue and beauty are the products of artifice; yet we remember the famous and exquisite sonnet in which he speaks of Nature as a temple up-borne on living pillars, as a "forest of symbols", full of strange meanings for the poet who wanders through its avenues. Such contradictions need not unduly dismay us. Poets differ from philosophers in so far as they recognise that a conflict, even a confusion, of ideas, if accurately reflected and honestly reproduced, may be as revelatory as a hard-and-fast system achieved by ruthless intellectual pruning; and Baudelaire's poetic character was a synthesis of contradictory impulses.

"Tout enfant", he wrote in *Mon Coeur Mis a Nu* ('My Heart laid Bare'), *"j'ai senti dans mon coeur deux sentiments contradictoires, l'horreur de la vie et l'extase de la vie."* The strength of these feelings never declined; nor did the conflict lose its violence. Baudelaire's collected works show us a man who hates and fears life, and hates and despises the conditions of modern society; who is oppressed by an *"immense nausée d'affiches"*, and who wonders that an honest man can touch a newspaper without an instinctive movement of repulsion; but who is fascinated by the beauty that lies in squalor, the energy that he seems to distinguish flowering in evil; whose attitude towards the world and his fellow human-beings is swayed by alternate impulses of rejection and acceptance. He has an invincible yearning for the life of the spirit, and opens *Fusées* ('Rockets'), with the affirmation: *"Quand même Dieu n'existerait pas, la religion serait encore sainte et divine";* but had Baudelaire been by temperament the ascetic that he often wished to be, had he never penetrated those wildernesses of sensual experience where he lost health and happiness and ordinary peace of mind, what his character gained in dignity his imagination would have forfeited in richness and variety. On the one hand, he is an impassioned puritan, with a puritan's distaste for Woman (whom he regards as the natural enemy of the dandy, saint or artist); on the other, he drifts into profound reveries suggested by his mistress' sensual grace, and is a

delighted observer of the contemporary social scene, enamoured of the *"beauté de circonstance"*, *"le beau multiforme et versicolore qui se meut dans les spirales infinies de la vie"*, a beauty he finds in clothes and equipages, in *"quelque chose d'ardent et de triste"* he glimpses in the face of an unknown passer-by, in the tide of urban prostitution which, as dusk falls and the gas-jets flutter and rustle under the wind, begins to creep like an invading army along the crowded greasy pavements.

To gather and convey these impressions, and maintain all the while a delicate equipoise between impulses of love and hatred, demands of the poet-critic an extremely arduous training. Though accounted by his family, and sometimes by himself, a wastrel and an idler, Baudelaire devoted prodigious application to the literary task before him. But his disappointments were numerous and crushing, his humiliations exquisite; and, as hope declined, a disease, contracted during early manhood, which he believed that he had overcome, gradually reappeared with new and ominous symptoms. He understood that he was threatened by mental collapse. *"Aujourd'hui "*, he noted, *"23 janvier 1862, j'ai subi un singulier avertissement, j'ai senti passer en moi le vent de l'aile de l'imbécillité."* The beat of those dreadful wings grew steadily louder and more terrifying. Baudelaire left Paris for Brussels in April, 1864. There he delivered a series of unrewarding lectures, and began to write *Mon Coeur mis à Nu*, the critical and autobiographical volume, which, if he had ever completed it, he intended to hurl down as his final challenge to society. He would have liked, he told his long-suffering and uncomprehending mother, to rouse the whole human race against him. But neither energy nor time was left; the book remained a collection of revelatory fragments, essential to our understanding of the author's life and character, mixed with brief personal jottings and suggestions for unwritten essays.

In 1866 he experienced a complete collapse, and during the summer of that year his friends brought him back to Paris. He lingered on another twelve months, a partially paralysed and nearly speechless derelict.

At a first glance, the facts of Baudelaire's biography seem tragically simple. The only son of an elderly man and a devout, well-brought-up young woman, he had loved his mother as a child with a fierce, possessive passion, and could never forgive the wound inflicted on his youthful sensibility by Madame Baudelaire's second marriage to the dashing General Aupick. Henceforward there existed in his mind a gulf, which he could rarely bridge, between sensual and spiritual love: the woman he loved spiritually (as he loved his mother in his childhood, and as he was later to love the mysterious "Marie" and that jovial and commonplace personage Madame Sabatier) he found it difficult to approach physically: the earthly Venus, personified in his mulatto mistress, Jeanne Duval, was seductive and imaginatively stimulating but necessarily abject.

Few men have "warred against their fortune" with more ingenious obstinacy: juvenile dissipations cost him his health, and early extravagances deprived him of a modest private income. From the burden of debt he could never escape; and though he did not hesitate to appeal to his mother's generosity, he could never learn to accept her help without an embittered sense of shame. Both sorrow and pleasure dealt him their heaviest blows; and on the eve of his departure for Brussels, at a time when he had not reached his forty-third birthday, he is described as looking already prematurely aged—an impression that is confirmed by Nadar's well-known photograph. His hair is thin, and his cheeks are deeply furrowed; the hard line of the mouth is clamped down like a box-lid; but the sunk eyes still glitter with saturnine intelligence. The face of a man whom life had apparently broken; but there was that in his genius which brought order from confusion, and built success on failure. The eccentric colonist of a literary Kamtchatka now strikes us as having occupied a dominant position in the history of modern European writing. Where Romanticism ended, and the Romantic dream faded into the prosaic reality of mid-nineteenth century Europe, it was Baudelaire's mission and fate to raise his intellectual standard.

THE PAINTER OF MODERN LIFE (*)

I

BEAUTY, FASHION AND HAPPINESS

THERE are educated people, and even artists, who when visiting the Louvre Museum pass rapidly and without a glance by rows of pictures that are highly interesting, although of the second rank, and station themselves in rapture before a Titian or Raphael—one of those pictures that have been especially popularised by the art of the engraver. Then they go away satisfied, many a one reflecting how well he knows his Louvre. Similarly there are people who, because they have in their time read Bossuet and Racine, believe themselves to be well-versed in the history of literature.

Fortunately there come on the scene from time to time the men to right such wrongs: critics, art-lovers and keen students, who point out that Raphael is not everything, nor Racine either; that lesser craftsmen have much that is good, solid and delightful; and finally that a love of universal beauty, as expressed by the classical poets and artists, is no excuse for ignoring particular beauty—the beauty of the occasion, and of day-to-day existence.

* "It is common knowledge that the person referred to is Mr. Constantin Guys, whose beautiful water- colours are known to, and are eagerly sought by, art-lovers and artists. The following pages will explain the motives, of delicacy and deference, that caused Baudelaire to refrain from naming his friend, in this study of his work, otherwise than by his initials. In the text we have respected Charles Baudelaire's obliging kindness, and have claimed a historian's rights only in this footnote." *Note by Messrs. Calmann-Lévy, publishers of: Charles Baudelaire: Oeuvres Complètes.*

I should add that during the last few years society has slightly improved in this respect. The value attached by art-lovers nowadays to the charming coloured reproductions of the eighteenth century shows that there has been a highly desirable public reaction. Debucourt, the Saint-Aubins and many others are now listed in the dictionaries as artists deserving study.

But these artists depict the past; and today I wish to concern myself with the depiction of contemporary life. The past is interesting not only for the beauty distilled from it by the artists to whom it was the present, but also because it is past—for its historical value. The same is true of the present. The pleasure we derive from the depiction of the present arises not only from the beauty in which it can be attired, but also from its essential quality of being the present.

I have before me a series of reproductions of fashion-drawings, starting at the Revolution and ending almost at the Consulate. The costumes here depicted, which seem ridiculous to thoughtless people—those people who are so serious because they lack true seriousness—have a double charm, both artistic and historical. They are very often attractive and intelligently drawn; but what to me is at least as important, and what I am happy to find in all or almost all of them, is an understanding of the spirit and the aesthetic values of their period. A man's idea of what is beautiful imprints itself upon all his attire and bearing; it crumples or smoothes his coat, rounds out or straightens his movements, and in time subtly penetrates even his features. A man ends by resembling what he would like to be.

These reproductions can be regarded either as handsome or as ugly; if the latter, they become caricatures; if the former, they are like antique statues.

The women who wore these costumes resembled one another more or less closely, in accordance with the various degrees of poetic sensibility or of vulgarity with which they were endowed. Their living substance puts movement into what to us seems too rigid. The spectator's imagination can still today see the stir and hear the rustle of this tunic or that shawl.

One of these days, perhaps, some theatre will show a play in which we shall behold a resurrection of those costumes in which our ancestors thought themselves just as fascinating as we think ourselves in *our* poor garments—which also have, it is true, their own grace, but more of a moral and spiritual description; and if these costumes are worn and lent animation by intelligent actresses and actors, we shall be astonished at ourselves for having been able to laugh so fatuously. The past, whilst retaining the fascination of a ghost, will regain the light and movement of life, and will become the present.

If an impartial person were to scan, one by one, *all* French fashions, from the nation's beginnings to the present day, he would find nothing shocking, or even surprising, about any of them. The transitions from one to another would be as elaborately detailed as in the world of biology. There would be no gaps, and therefore no surprises. And if, when contemplating the sketch depicting any particular period, he were also to recall the philosophy which especially influenced or disturbed that period, he would see what a profound harmony prevails between all the various branches of history; and that, even during the centuries which to us seem the maddest and most monstrous, the deathless appetite for beauty has always found its satisfaction.

This would, indeed, be an excellent opportunity to build a rational and historical theory of beauty, in opposition to the theory of a beauty that is single and absolute; to show that beauty, although it makes but a single impression, always and inevitably contains two elements; for the difficulty of discerning, behind the singleness of the impression, the separate elements that go to its making, does not at all invalidate the fact that more than a single element must be there. Beauty is composed of one element that is eternal, invariable and exceedingly difficult to assess, and of another element that is relative and a product of circumstance. This latter element may be described as being, either severally or jointly, the period, its fashions, its morals and its appetites. Without this second element, which is, so to speak the amusing, stimulating, appetising icing on the divine cake, the first element would be indigestible and beyond our powers of appreciation; unadapted and unsuitable to human nature. I defy anyone to discover any particle of beauty that does not contain both these elements.

I can select if desired two examples from the extreme ends of the scale of history. In religious art the duality I have described can be seen at a glance: the element of eternal beauty discloses itself only by the permission and under the direction of the religion that the artist professes. And, likewise, even in the most frivolous productions of a sensitive artist belonging to one of these periods that we vaingloriously describe as civilised, the duality is equally apparent; the eternal element is both veiled and expressed, either by contemporary fashion or at least by the author's personal temperament.

The duality of art is an inevitable result of the duality of human nature. You may, if you wish, regard the eternally existing element as the soul of art, and the changeable element as its body. That is why Stendhal—an impertinent, teasing and even unpleasant writer, but one whose impertinences usefully stimulate reflection—came nearer to the truth than many other people when he observed that: "Beauty is only the promise of happiness." This definition certainly overshoots the mark: it places beauty too much in subjection to the infinitely variable concept of happiness, and too lightly robs beauty of its aristocratic quality. But it has the great merit of distinctly departing from the error of the academicians.

I have explained all this more than once before, and what I have written here is sufficient for those who enjoy playing with abstractions; but I know that most French readers are not very fond of this sport, and I myself am eager to pass on to the positive and particular part of my theme.

II

SKETCHES OF CONTEMPORARY SCENES

For sketches of contemporary scenes, for the depiction of the life of the citizen and the pageantry of fashion, obviously the best method is that which is quickest and least costly. The more beauty the artist puts into them, the more valuable his work will be; but there is in ordinary life, in the daily metamorphoses of outward appearances, a rapid movement that demands from the artist an equal speed of execution.

Eighteenth-century engravings in several colours have, as I was saying just now, come back into fashion. Pastels, etchings and aquatints have in turn contributed their quotas to the immense dictionary of modern life that is scattered through bookshops and art-lovers' portfolios, and behind the windows of the cheapest stores. As soon as lithography made its appearance, it at once proved to be highly suited for this enormous and seemingly frivolous task.

This class of work has provided us with real monuments. The works of Gavarni and Daumier have justly been described as complementary to the *Comédie humaine*. Balzac himself, I am convinced, would not have been disinclined to adopt this idea, which is all the more accurate in that the artist who paints contemporary scenes is a genius of mixed nature—that is to say, a genius with a considerable component of literary ability. Observer, idle looker-on, philosopher, call him what you will, you are certainly obliged, when describing such an artist, to use a term that you could not apply to the painter of eternal, or at any rate more lasting, subjects such as those of history or religion. Sometimes he is a poet; more often he has a kinship with the novelist or the moralist; he is the painter of the occasion, and also of all its suggestions of the eternal.

Every country, to its pleasure and glory, has possessed a few such men. At the present time, in addition to Daumier and Gavarni (the first names that one recalls) one may mention Devéria, Maurin, Numa, (recorders of the usurpatory graces of the Restoration), Eugène Lami (the last-named almost English in his love of the aristocratic elegances) and even Trimolet and Travies, those chroniclers of poverty and restricted lives.

III

ARTIST, MAN OF THE WORLD,
MAN OF THE MASSES, CHILD

I wish today to entertain my readers with an account of a remarkable man, of such powerful and distinct originality that it is sufficient unto itself and does not even seek applause. None of his drawings is signed—if by a signature one means those few alphabetical characters, so easy to counterfeit, that spell out a name and are solemnly appended by so many other artists to their most casual sketches. But all his works bear the signature of his brilliant soul; and art-lovers who have seen and appreciated them will easily recognise them by the description that I propose to give.

Deeply in love with the masses, and also with anonymity, Mr. C. G. pushes originality to the point of bashfulness. Mr. Thackeray, who, as is well known, is a keen student of artistic matters, and himself draws the illustrations for his novels, once referred to Mr. G. in a little-read London periodical. Mr. G. was vexed as if by an outrage upon his modesty. Again, more recently, when he learnt that I proposed to write an appreciation of his personality and talent, he besought me most imperiously to suppress his name, and to speak of his works only as those of an unknown artist.

I shall humbly fall in with this bizarre wish. We shall pretend to believe, the reader and I, that Mr. G. does not exist, and we shall concern ourselves with his drawings and water-colours, for which he professes a patrician contempt, as if we were scholars passing judgment on some valuable historic documents that have been found by chance and whose author must always be unknown. Nay, more, completely to ease my conscience, we shall suppose that all I have to say concerning his character, so curiously and mysteriously brilliant, has been suggested, with greater or less accuracy, by his work alone; that it is all poetical supposition, conjecture, a product of my imagination.

Mr. G. is elderly. Jean-Jacques began writing, it is said, at the age of forty-two. It was perhaps at about the same age that Mr. G., obsessed with all the images in his head, had the audacity to lay ink and colours on a white page. If the truth must be told, he drew like a barbarian or a child, struggling angrily against the clumsiness of his fingers and the disobedience of his instrument. I have seen a great number of these primitive daubs, and I confess that most of the people who know, or claim to know, about such matters could have failed, without disgrace to themselves, to recognise the genius latent in these murky scribbles. Today Mr. G., after discovering entirely by himself all the little tricks of the trade, has become a powerful master in his own style, and has retained of his first ingenuousness only what is required to lend to his rich gifts an unexpected extra flavour. When he comes across one of the first attempts of his "youth", he tears them up or burns them with a comical shamefacedness.

For ten years I wished to make the acquaintance of Mr. G., who is by nature very much a traveller and a cosmopolitan. I knew that for a long time he had worked for an English illustrated magazine, which had published reproductions of his travel sketches (Spain, Turkey, the Crimea). Since then I have seen a considerable quantity of these drawings, hastily executed on the spot, and have thus been able to "read" a detailed and day-by-day account, much better than any other, of the Crimean campaign.

The same magazine had also published—always without a signature—numerous other compositions by the same author, taken from new ballets and operas. When at last I met him, the first thing I realised was that here was not exactly an *artist*, but rather a *man of the world*.

I beg you to understand here the word "artist" in a very narrow sense, and the words "man of the world" in their widest sense. Man of the world—that means a man of the world as a whole, a man who understands the world and the mysterious yet legitimate reasons for all its habits. Artist—that means a specialist, a man bound to his palette as a serf is bound to his glebe. Mr. G. does not like to be called an artist. Is he not to some extent right? He is interested in the world as a whole; he wants to know, understand and appreciate everything that happens on the surface of this globe of ours.

The artist lives very little, or not at all, in the world of morals or of politics. He who lives in the Quartier Bréda does not know what is happening in the Faubourg Saint-Germain.

With two or three exceptions, which need not be named, most artists are, it must be confessed, simply very clever animals, pure artisans, with the intelligences and brains of the village or hamlet. Their conversation, which is necessarily restricted to a very small range of interests, quickly becomes intolerable to the "man of the world", that spiritual citizen of the universe.

To begin to understand Mr. G., therefore, you should first of all take note that what may be regarded as the mainspring of his genius is *a keen appreciation of life*.

Do you remember a picture (for indeed it is a picture!) composed by the most powerful writer of our time and entitled "l'Homme des foules".* From behind the window of a café a convalescent joyfully contemplates the crowd, and in imagination enters into all the thoughts that are going on around him. Recently returned from the shades of death, he delightedly breathes in all the germs and odours of life. Having been on the brink of entire forgetting, he now remembers, and eagerly wishes to remember, everything. Finally he rushes through the crowd in search of an unknown person, a glimpse of whose face has suddenly fascinated him. His keen appreciation of life has become a fatal and irresistible passion!

Imagine an artist whose spiritual condition is always that of this convalescent, and you will have the key to the character of Mr. G.

Now, convalescence is a sort of return to childhood. The convalescent enjoys, as the child does, the faculty of taking a lively interest in everything, even in the apparently most trivial things. Let us return, if we can, by a retrospective effort of the imagination, to our youngest, most matutinal impressions. We shall recognise that they had a remarkable affinity with the highly coloured impressions that we received, later on, after a physical illness—provided that this

* The man of the masses.

illness did no damage to our mental or spiritual faculties. For the child everything is *new;* he is always *exhilarated*. Nothing more closely resembles what is called inspiration than the joy of a child absorbing form and colour. I shall venture to go further, and assert that inspiration has something in common with cerebral congestion, and that every sublime thought is accompanied by a nervous shock, of greater or less violence, which reaches even the brain.

The nerves of the man of genius are strong; those of a child are weak. In the former reason plays a considerable role; in the latter almost the whole being is occupied by sensibility. Nevertheless, genius is simply *childhood rediscovered* by an act of will; childhood now endowed, for its self-expression, with the organs of a man and that analytical power that enables a man to put order into the automatically amassed sum of physical experiences.

This deep and joyful appreciation of life is the explanation of the fixed and animally ecstatic gaze of a child confronted by what is *new*--whatever it may be, a face or a landscape, light, gilding, colours, shot silks, the magic of a woman's beauty enhanced by her labours at the dressing-table.

A friend of mine once told me that when he was very small he used to watch his father dressing, and would gaze, in wonderment mixed with delight, at the muscles of the arms, the graduated shades of faint pink and yellow in the skin, and the bluish network of veins. The picture of life's outward appearances was already filling the child with deep respect, and laying hold of his very brain. Already he was obsessed and possessed by the contemplation of form. Predestination was precociously showing the tip of its nose. My friend's doom was sealed. Need I add that today this child is a well-known painter?

I was asking you just now to regard Mr. G. as a perpetual convalescent. To complete your notion of him, think of him also as a child-man, as a man possessing at every moment the genius of childhood—a genius, that is to say, for which no aspect of life has become stalely familiar.

I have told you that I was disinclined to call him an artist pure and simple, and that he himself rejected this title with a modesty tinged with aristocratic disdain. I would like to call him a "dandy," and would have good reasons to do so; for the word "dandy" implies a certain quintessence of character and a subtle understanding of the whole moral mechanism of human society. But, against this, the dandy aspires to indifference; and it is here that Mr. G., ruled as he is by an insatiable passion—the passion for seeing and feeling—violently breaks with dandyism. *"Amabam amare,"* said St. Augustine. I am passionately in love with passion, Mr. G. would readily admit. The dandy is indifferent, or feigns to be so, for reasons of policy and caste. Mr. G. has a horror of indifferent people. He is a master of the difficult art—people of sensibility will understand me—of *being sincere without being ridiculous*. I might well honour him with the title of philosopher, to which he has more than one claim, were it not that his excessive love of things visible, tangible and reduced to plastic form inspires him with a certain repugnance towards those things that constitute the impalpable realm of the metaphysician. So let us relegate him to the rank of a pure pictorial moralist, like La Bruyère.

The masses are his domain, as the air is the bird's and the sea the fish's. His passion is his profession—that of *wedding himself to the masses*. To the perfect spectator, the impassioned observer, it is an immense joy to make his domicile amongst numbers, amidst fluctuation and movement, amidst the fugitive and infinite. To be away from home, and yet to feel at home; to behold the world, to be in the midst of the world, and yet to remain hidden from the world—these are some of the minor pleasures of such independent, impassioned and impartial spirits, whom words can only clumsily describe.

The observer is a prince who always rejoices in his incognito. The lover of life makes the world his family, just as a lover of the fair sex enlists in his family all the beauties that he has captured, may capture or will never capture; or just as a lover of paintings lives in an enchanted society of dreams depicted on canvas. So the lover of the life of the universe enters into the masses as into a huge reservoir of electrical energy. He may also be compared to a mirror as huge as the masses themselves; to a kaleidoscope endowed with awareness, which at each of its movements reproduces the multiplicity of life and the restless grace of all life's elements. He is an *I* insatiably eager for the *not-I*, continually interpreting and expressing the latter in images more lovely than life itself, images always changing and fugitive.

"Any man," Mr. G. once said, in one of those conversations that he illuminates with his intense gaze and evocative gestures, "who is not stricken by an unrest so positive as to absorb all his faculties, and who *is capable of being bored in the bosom of a crowd*, any such man is a fool—a fool, and I despise him!"

When Mr. G wakes in the morning, opens his eyes and sees the rollicking sunlight beating on the squares of his windows, he thinks to himself remorsefully and regretfully: "What an imperious command! What a fanfare of light! Already for hours, now, there has been light everywhere— light wasted by my sleep! How many things I might have seen *in a new light*—and I did not see them!"

So he leaves his house, and watches the running river of life's essence, so majestic and so bright. He admires the eternal beauty and astonishing harmony of life in capital cities—a harmony still providentially preserved amidst the turbulence of human freedom. He contemplates the landscape of stone caressed by the mist or smacked by the sunlight. He rejoices in fine carriages, in proud horses, in the dazzling smartness of grooms, in the dexterity of servants, in the undulous gait of women, in the handsome children who are happy to be alive and well-dressed. He rejoices in life as a whole.

If a fashion or the cut of a garment has been slightly altered; if buckles or bunches of ribbons have been dethroned by rosettes; if women's caps have been enlarged, or the chignon has descended by a quarter of an inch upon the nape; if the waist has been raised and the skirt amplified—be sure that, from an enormous distance, his eagle's eye has already perceived it.

A regiment passes, on its way, perhaps, to the ends of the earth, filling the air of the boulevards with its fanfares as seductive and as fickle as hope—and behold, the eye of Mr. G. has already seen, inspected and analysed these troops' weapons, march-discipline and physique. Equipment, the glitter of metal, music, firm glances, heavy and serious moustaches—all these have entered pell-mell into him; and in a few minutes the resulting poem will virtually be already composed. And now his soul lives with the soul of that regiment, that proud image of delight in obedience.

But evening has come. It is the strange and suspect hour when the sky's curtains are drawn and the cities light up. The gas-light makes a stain upon the red of the sunset. Honest men and rogues, sane men and madmen, think to themselves: "At last the day is over." Worthy men and wicked men turn their thoughts to pleasure, and each of them hurries to the place of his choice, to drink the cup of forgetfulness. Mr. G. will be the last person remaining wherever light shines, poetry thunders, life teems, music throbs; wherever any human passion can "pose" for his inspection; wherever the natural man and the man of convention display themselves in a strange beauty; wherever the sun shines on the fleeting joys of that depraved animal, man.

"In sooth, a day well spent!" thinks a certain type of reader, whom we have all met. "Any of us has enough genius to fill his day in that fashion." No! Few men are gifted with the faculty of seeing, and still fewer have the power of expressing what they see. Now, at an hour when other men are asleep, Mr. G. is bent over his table, darting at a sheet of paper the same glance that shortly before was lingering upon all sorts of objects. He is at sword-play with his pencil, pen or brush; he makes the water in his glass spirtle to the ceiling; he wipes his pen on his shirt—eager, violent, busy, as if he feared that his images might escape him; cantankerous although alone, bullying himself onward.

And objects are reborn upon the paper, true to life and more than true to life, beautiful and more than beautiful, strange and endowed with an enthusiastic vitality, like the soul of their author. Out of nature has been distilled fantasy. All the stuffs with which memory is encumbered are classified and arranged in order, are harmonised and subjected to that compulsory formalisation which results from a *childish* perceptiveness—that is to say, a perceptiveness acute and magical by reason of its simplicity!

IV

MODERNITY

Thus he goes his way, hurrying and seeking. What does he seek? It is certain that this man, such a one as I have described, this solitary gifted with an active imagination, and always travelling across the great human desert, has a higher aim than any mere idle spectator—a more general aim, something else than the fleeting pleasures of the occasion.

This "something else" that he seeks is what we may

be allowed to call "modernity"; for there is no better word to express the idea behind it. His business is to separate from contemporary fashion whatever it may contain of poetry within history; to extract the eternal from the ephemeral.

If we cast an eye over the usual exhibitions of modern paintings, we are struck by the artists' general tendency to clothe all their subjects in the costumes of antiquity. Almost all of them use the fashions and furnishings of the Renaissance, just as David used the modes and furnishings of ancient Rome. There is, however, this difference: that David, having selected specifically Greek or Roman themes, could do no otherwise than array them in ancient style; whereas the painters of the day, whilst selecting themes of a general nature, applicable to all periods, insist on rigging them out in costumes of the Middle Ages, the Renaissance or the East. This is clearly a sign of great laziness; for it is much more convenient to declare that the dress of a period is entirely ugly than to apply oneself to distilling from it whatever mysterious beauty it may contain, however minimal or fleeting.

Modernity is that which is ephemeral, fugitive, contingent upon the occasion; it is half of art, whose other half is the eternal and unchangeable.

Every old-time painter had his own modernity; most of the lovely portraits that have come down to us from bygone times are clad in the costumes of their various periods. They are perfectly harmonious, because the costume, the coiffure, and even the gesture, the glance and the smile (every period has its own deportment, glance and smile) compose a whole that has a complete truth to life.

This ephemeral and fugitive element, subject to so frequent metamorphoses, is not to be despised or ignored. By disregarding it, you necessarily fall into the void of a beauty abstract and indefinable, such beauty as that one woman must have had who lived before the first sin was committed. If, for the correct and inevitable costume of a given period, you substitute another, you are creating an anomaly such as could be excused only in some fashionable masquerade. (For example, the goddesses, nymphs and sultanas of the eighteenth century are portraits *morally* in keeping with their time).

It is beyond doubt an excellent thing to study the Old Masters in order to learn how to paint; but this can only be a subsidiary exercise, if your purpose is to understand the nature of beauty in the present time. The draperies of Rubens or Veronese will not teach you to depict *moiré antique* or *satin à la reine* or any other stuff of modern manufacture that is designed to be supported and carried on a crinoline or on starched muslin petticoats. The weave and grain are not the same as in the stuffs of ancient Venice, or in those worn at the court of Catherine. Furthermore, the cut of the petticoat or the bodice itself is completely different; the pleats are arranged in a new system; and, lastly, the gestures and carriage of the woman herself give her gown a life and physical existence which are not those of the robe of the woman of antiquity.

In short, in order that any particular modernity may be worthy of eventually becoming antiquity, it is necessary that the mysterious beauty involuntarily lent to it by human life should be distilled from it. This is the task to which Mr. G. especially applies himself.

I have said that every period has its deportment, its glance and its gesture. This statement can be verified with especial ease in any vast portrait-gallery, such as that of Versailles. But it has a still wider application. In any of those unities known as nations, professions or classes, the passing centuries introduce a variety not only of gestures and manners, but also of actual facial features. Particular types of nose, mouth and forehead occupy given spaces of time which I shall not endeavour to determine here, but which could certainly be made a subject of exact calculation.

Portrait-painters are insufficiently aware of all this; and the great fault of Mr. Ingres, in particular, is that he tries to impose upon every type that comes before his easel a more or less despotic idea of perfection, borrowed from the classical repertory.

On such a question it would be easy, and indeed permissible, to argue *a priori*. The perpetual correlation between what is called "the soul" and what is called "the body" shows quite clearly how all that is material, or in other words a pro-jection of the spiritual, reflects and always will reflect the spiritual from which it derives. If a painter who is patient and scrupulous, but of mediocre powers of imagination, has the task of painting a contemporary courtesan and "takes his inspiration" (this is the accepted phrase) from a courtesan by Titian or Raphael, it is very highly probable that his work will be false, ambiguous and obscure. Studying a masterpiece dealing with a similar subject, but in bygone times, will not teach him the attitude, the facial expression, the grimaces or the living aspect of one of those creatures whom the dictionary of fashion has successively classified under the coarse or facetious titles of "fallen" or "kept" women, "gay girls" or "tarts".

The same criticism can be strictly applied to the depiction of the soldier or the dandy, or even of animals such as dogs or horses; indeed, of everything that goes to make up the outward appearances of an epoch. Woe on him who seeks in the study of antiquity anything but pure art, logic and general method! By immersing himself too long in the past, he loses his memory of the present; he surrenders the values and privileges supplied by circumstance; for almost all our originality comes from the stamp that *time* imprints upon our perceptions.

The reader will understand, without my telling him, that I could easily support these statements in regard to the depiction of many other things besides women. What would you say, for example, (I offer an extreme case), of a painter of naval subjects who, when called upon to depict the sober and elegant beauty of a modern ship-of-the-line, were to weary his eyes with studying the overloaded and convoluted outlines and monumental stern of an old galleon, or the complicated heads-of-sail of the sixteenth century? Or what would you think of an artist whom you had commissioned to portray a blood-horse famous in the solemn annals of the turf, if he were to confine his researches to the museums, and to content himself with studying the horse in the galleries of the past—in Van Dyck, Bourgignon or Van der Meulen?

Mr. G., under a natural compulsion and the tyranny of circumstance, has followed a quite different path. He began by observing life, and only later did he set himself to learn the methods of depicting it. The result has been an enthralling originality, in which any relic of barbarism or ingenuousness appears as a further proof of his faithfulness to the impressions he has received—as a compliment paid to truth.

For most of us, and especially for men of affairs, in whose eyes nature has no existence except in its utilitarian relations to their business, the fantastic reality of life has been remarkably staled by use. Mr. G., on the other hand, takes it in unceasingly; his memory and his eyes are full of it.

V

BARBARISM

This word "barbarism," which has been slipping off my pen perhaps too often, might make some reader think that we are dealing here with a few rude sketches that can be transformed into perfected work only by the imagination of the beholder. This would be a misunderstanding of what I mean. I am speaking of a barbarism that is necessary, synthesising and childish; a barbarism of which traces can often be seen in a perfected art—Mexican, Egyptian or Ninevite, for example—a barbarism derived from the need to see things largely, to view them primarily in connection with their surroundings.

It is worth while mentioning here that accusations of barbarism have often been levelled against all those painters whose view of objects is synthesising and simplifying: Mr. Corot, for example, who sets himself primarily to trace the chief outlines of a landscape—its bone-structure and physiognomy. So Mr. G., faithfully interpreting his own impressions, instinctively emphasises the focal or luminous parts of an object (they may be the *dramatically* focal or luminous parts) or its chief characteristics—sometimes even with an exaggeration that is useful as a prompter to the human memory; so that the imagination of the beholder, coming under the sway of these masterful reminders, clearly sees the impression made by this or the other object on the mind of Mr. G. The beholder is thus the interpreter of an interpretation that is always brilliant and exhilarating.

This is a state of affairs that greatly adds to the living force of this *legendary* rendering of life's outward appearances. I wish now to describe Mr. G.'s method of drawing. He draws from memory, not from a model—except when, as in the Crimean War, it was urgently necessary to take immediate and hasty notes, in order to fix the subject's chief outlines. (Indeed, all true draughtsmen draw from an image in their brains, and not from nature. If anyone quotes against me the admirable sketches of Raphael, Watteau and many others, I shall reply that these are notes—minutely detailed, it is true, but simply notes.)

When a true artist has arrived at the stage of final execution of a work, a model would be more a hindrance than a help to him. It even happens that men like Daumier and Mr. G., long accustomed to using their memory and to filling it with images, find, when confronted with the model and its multiplicity of detail, that their chief faculty is disturbed and, as it were, paralysed.

There is thus set up a struggle between the will to see everything and forget nothing, and the memorising faculty, which has become accustomed actively to absorb general colours, silhouettes and all the arabesques of contour. An artist who has a perfected feeling for form, but is accustomed primarily to exercise this memory and imagination, finds himself assailed, so to speak, by an insurgent mob of details all demanding justice with the fury of a crowd in love with absolute equality. The result is that all justice is violated and all harmony sacrificed and destroyed. Many a triviality assumes enormous importance, many a commoner usurps a throne. The more the artist gives impartial heed to all details, the more anarchy increases. Be he short-sighted or long-sighted, all traces of hierarchy and subordination disappear.

This is an accident that often occurs in the works of one of our most fashionable painters (a man whose weaknesses, by the way, are so well in tune with those of the masses that they have made a remarkable contribution to his popularity).

The same analogy can be discovered in the practice of the actor's art, that deep and mysterious art which today has fallen into such a confusion of decadence. Mr. Frédérick-Lemaître creates a part with the sweep and amplitude of genius. However spangled his performance may be with luminous details, it is always synthesising and sculptural. Mr. Bouffé, on the other hand, creates a part with the minute care of a myopic or a bureaucrat. Everything in his performance is brilliant, but nothing can be seen, nothing insists on remaining in one's memory.

In Mr. G.'s execution of his work, then, two things are evident: the first, the exertion of a resurrective, evocative memory, which bids every object: "Lazarus, arise!"; the second, a fiery exhilaration of the pencil and brush, almost resembling an outburst of mania.

It is the fear of not being fast enough, of letting the phantom escape before its essence has been distilled and captured; it is this terrible fear that possesses all great artists, and makes them desire so ardently to gain mastery of all the means of expression—so that the commands of the mind may never be distorted by the hesitations of the hand; so that finally the act of execution, the ideal act of execution, may become as unconscious and spontaneous as, say, the process of digestion seems to a healthy man after dinner.

Mr. G. begins with a few light touches of the pencil, which scarcely do more than indicate the places that the various objects are to occupy within the framework. Next the chief planes are indicated by wash-tints—vague masses of faint colour at first, but later on retouched and loaded with colours successively more intense. Only at the last moment are the outlines of the various objects definitely marked in ink.

Nobody who has not seen his work could imagine what surprising effects Mr. G. can obtain by this simple, almost elementary, method. It has this incomparable advantage, that at any stage of a picture's making it looks sufficiently finished. You may perhaps say, at such-and-such a stage, that it is just a sketch; but it will be a perfect sketch. All its values are harmonious; and if Mr. G. chooses to carry them further they will march steadily abreast towards the sought-for perfection.

In this way he prepares twenty drawings at a time, with a charming petulance and delight that even he himself finds amusing. The sketches pile up in tens, in hundreds, in thousands. Now and then he looks through them, examining them carefully, picks out a few and makes greater or lesser additions to their intensity, darkening the shades and progressively brightening the highlights.

He attaches immense importance to his backgrounds, which, whether bold or faint, are always of a quality and nature appropriate to the figures. Scale of tones and general harmony are strictly observed, with a genius arising more from instinct than from study. For Mr. G. naturally possesses that mysterious talent of the colorist, a real gift which can perhaps be increased by study, but is, I think, in itself impossible to create.

To put it all in a sentence, our strange artist depicts at the same time the gestures and attitudes, whether magnificent or grotesque, of living creatures, and also their brilliant explosion in space.

VI

WAR-SKETCHES

Bulgaria, Turkey, the Crimea and Spain were feasts of spectacle to Mr. G.—or, rather, to the imaginary artist whom we have agreed to call Mr. G. For I now and then remember that I promised myself, the better to comfort his modesty, that I would suppose him to be non-existent. I have perused his archives of the war in the East: battlefields strewn with funeral debris, ammunition-carts, embarkations of cattle and horses—pictures living and enthralling, hewn from the stuff of life itself, with elements of pictorial value that many renowned painters, if placed in the same circumstances, would have blindly neglected; with the exception, which I gladly make, of M. Horace Vernet, who is really a chronicler more than essentially a painter, and with whom Mr. G., although a more delicate artist, has obvious points in common; if, that is to say, one considers the latter, too, only as a keeper of life's records.

I can affirm that no newspaper report, narrative or book expresses so well, in all its painful detail and sinister grandeur, the great epic of the Crimean War. Your eye travels, in turn, along the banks of the Danube, the shores of the Bosphorus, to Cape Kherson over the plain of Bala-clava, over the field of Inkerman, over the English, French, Turkish and Piedmontese camps, through the streets of Constantinople, through hospitals and solemn religious or military ceremonies.

One of the best reproduced of these compositions, to my mind, is the "Consecration of the burial-ground at Scutari by the Bishop of Gibraltar." The scene's picturesqueness, which consists in the contrast between the oriental environ-ment and the occidental attitudes and uniforms of the officiants, is presented in a striking and suggestive manner, rich in food for thought. The soldiers and officers have that imperishable air of "gentlemen", resolute and discreet, which they carry to the ends of the earth—to the colonial garrisons of the Cape and the cantonments of India. The English priests dimly call to mind beadles or stockbrokers in birettas and bands.

Next we are at Schumla, in the home of Omar Pasha: Turkish hospitality, hookahs and coffee. All the visitors are ranged on divans, putting to their lips pipes as long as speaking-tubes, whose bases are on the floor at their feet.

And here, now, are the "Kurds at Scutari", strange troops whose appearance makes one dream of an invasion by barbarian hordes. And here are the bashi-bazouks, no less strange in contrast with their European officers—Hungarians or Poles, whose dandified appearance stands out oddly from amongst their baroquely oriental soldiers.

Here I find a magnificent drawing, a full-length of a single personage, tall and robust, with an air at once pensive, careless and bold; big boots reach above his knees; his military uniform is hidden by a huge, heavy cape, precisely buttoned up; he is gazing through the smoke of his cigar at a sinister, misty horizon; he is wounded in one arm, which is supported in a sling. Underneath I read the words, scribbled in pencil: "Canrobert on the battle-field of Inkerman. Taken on the spot." *

And now who is this horseman with a white moustache and vigorously lined features? His head is thrown back, and he seems to be inhaling the terrible poetry of a field of battle; whilst his horse, with head drooping, picks its way amongst piles of corpses, which lie in strange attitudes, with feet sticking up into the air and convulsed faces. Beneath the drawing, in a corner, the words can be read: "Myself at Inkerman."

Here I see M. Baraguay-d'Hilliers, accompanied by le Seraskier, inspecting artillery at Bechichtash. Seldom have I seen a military portrait that gave a better likeness, or was limned by a bolder and wittier hand.

Next I come upon a name that has gained a sinister fame since the disasters in Syria: "Ahmed Pasha, G.O.C. at Kalafat, in front of his hut with his staff, being introduced to two European officers." Despite the size of his Turkish belly, Ahmed Pasha's face and bearing have that great air of aristocracy that is commonly found amongst the ruling races.

The battle of Balaclava is depicted several times. Here is one of the most striking scenes: the historic cavalry charge sung by the heroic trumpet of Alfred Tennyson, poet to the Queen. A mass of horsemen is riding at prodigious speed amidst clouds of artillery-smoke, towards the horizon. In the background the landscape is enclosed by a line of green hills.

Here and there the eye, saddened by all this chaos of

* In English in the original.

gunfire, this lethal turbulence, lights with relief on pictures of religious scenes. English soldiers of various arms, amongst whom stand out the picturesque uniforms of kilted Scots, are assembled whilst an English priest conducts the Sunday service. His pulpit is three drums, two of them supporting the third.

Indeed, it is difficult for a mere pen to give a rendering of this huge and complicated poem of a thousand sketches, or to express the exhilaration one derives from all this pictorial beauty, often painful but never lachrymose, collected on some hundreds of pages whose stains and rents tell, in their own fashion, of the distress and tumult in the midst of which the artist jotted down his memories of each day. In the evening the army post took off to London Mr. G.'s notes and drawings. Often he would entrust to a single post more than ten sketches hastily drawn on onion-skin paper, for which the engravers and the subscribers to his magazine were waiting impatiently.

Sometimes these drawings depict ambulances, in which the very atmosphere seems sick, sad and heavy; every bed holds a separate pain. Sometimes they show the hospital at Pera. Here I see, talking with two nurses, who are as tall, pale and erect as figures by Le Sueur, a casually-dressed visitor, described by the bizarre legend: "My humble self." *

Here again, on rugged winding paths strewn with debris from a battle that is already ancient history, are mules and horses slowly carrying at their flanks, in big sling-chairs, the livid and motionless wounded. Elsewhere, across huge, snowy plains, camels with majestic breasts and heads carry provisions and munitions of every kind. Here is a whole world at war, teeming with life, busy and silent. And here are camps—bazaars littered with scraps of every sort of furniture, like barbarian villages improvised for the occasion. Through the barracks, along these rocky or snowy roads,

* In English in the original.

through these ravines pass the uniforms of several nations, all more or less war-torn or modified by the addition of pelisses and heavy boots.

It is a pity that this album, now dispersed in several quarters, its precious pages having been retained by the blockmakers to whom they were sent or by the editorial staff of *The Illustrated London News* should never have been shown to the Emperor. I think that he would have been much interested, and not a little moved, had he perused this narrative of the activities and bearing of his troops—from the most brilliant military feats to the most trivial occupations of ordinary life—depicted day after day, with scrupulous care, by this firm and intelligent hand of an artist and soldier.

VII

POMPS AND CEREMONIES

Turkey provided dear G. with many other admirable themes for his compositions: Bairam festivities—heavy, torrential splendours, in whose background appears, like a pale sun, the permanent boredom of the now defunct Sultan. Aligned on the sovereign's left are all his civic officials; on his right, his military staff, chief of which is Said Pasha, now Sultan of Egypt, then in attendance at Constantinople.

We see processions of ceremonial pomp heading for the little mosque adjacent to the palace. Amongst these crowds are Turkish functionaires, real caricatures of decadence, crushing their magnificent horses beneath the weight of their fantastic obesity.

We see massive carriages, like coaches of the time of Louis XIV, but gilded and adorned with Oriental super-fluity; out of these dart strange, feminine glances, through the strictly prescribed slits left for the eyes in the muslin veils.

We see dances of tumblers of the "third sex." Balzac's comical expression was never more applicable than to these: under the tremor of the swaying lights, the agitation of the flowing garments, the vivid fard upon cheeks, eyelids and eyebrows, or amidst the long tresses streaming down to the loins, you would find it difficult, if not impossible, to guess that these creatures were men.

We see, lastly, the women of the world of gallantry (if it is possible to use this word in connection with the East): usually Hungarians, Wallachians, Jewesses, Poles, Greeks and Armenians—for under a despotic government it is the oppressed races, and especially those which have to suffer the most, that supply the most numerous objects of prostitution. Some of these women have retained their national costumes—embroidered blouses, short sleeves, enveloping scarves, huge trousers, slippers turned up at the toes, striped or spangled muslin and all the tinsel of their native country; others, and these the more numerous, have adopted the chief sign of civilisation (which, for a woman, is invariably the crinoline), whilst yet retaining, in some part of their attire, some slight characteristic reminder of the East, so that they look like Parisian women in fancy dress.

Mr. G. excels at painting the pageantry of officialdom, its national pomps and ceremonies. He does this not coldly and didactically, like painters who see in such works nothing else than lucrative set-tasks, but with all the ardour of a man in love with space, with perspective, with light that comes in floods or sharp bursts, attaching itself in drops or sparkles to the severe uniforms and gowns of a court.

An interesting example of his talent for such work is "Independence Day Memorial Celebration in Athens Cathedral." All these little human figures, each so appropriate in its place, gives an added depth to the space surrounding them. The cathedral is huge, and is decorated with ceremonial hangings. King Otho and the Queen, standing on a platform, are dressed in traditional costume, which they wear with a marvellous naturalness, as if to attest the sincerity of their adoption and the most delicate Hellenic patriotism. The King's waist is strapped-in like that of the trimmest palikar, and his kilt flares out with all the exaggeration of the national dandyism. Opposite the Royal Pair the Patriarch advances—an old man with rounded shoulders and a big, white beard. His little eyes are shielded by green spectacles, and his whole being bears the signs of a consummately Oriental placidity.

All the human figures peopling the composition are portraits. One of the oddest of them—because of the unexpectedness of its appearance, which is entirely un-Hellenic— is that of a German lady, who sits by the Queen and is in waiting upon her.

In collections of Mr. G.'s work one often finds the French Emperor, whose features he has succeeded in reducing, without spoiling the likeness, to an infallible prototype, which he reproduces with the certainty of a set of scribbled initials. Sometimes the Emperor is carrying out an inspection at a gallop, accompanied by his officers, whose features can easily be recognised, or by foreign princes, European, Asiatic, or African, for whom he is, so to speak, doing the honours of, Paris. Sometimes he is sitting motionless on a horse, whose legs are as steady as the four legs of a table, with the Empress on his left, in Amazon costume, and on his right the little Imperial Prince, loaded down beneath a busby and sitting on a little horse as shaggy as the ponies that English artists so freely scatter about their landscapes. Sometimes the Emperor is disappearing in an eddy of light and dust along the avenues of the Bois de Boulogne; at other times he is passing at a walk amidst the applause of the Faubourg Saint-Antoine.

One of these water-colours, especially, astounded me with its magic. In the front of a box at the theatre, adorned with a heavy and regal wealth of decoration, the Empress can be seen in an attitude of tranquillity and repose; the Emperor is slightly stooping forward, as if to have a better look round the theatre. Standing over the Royal Pair, two guardsmen, of a military and almost liturgical immobility, reflect on their brilliant uniforms the spattering glare of the footlights. Beyond this field of fire, in the idyllic atmosphere of the stage, the actors are harmoniously singing, declaiming and posturing; on the near side extends an abyss of dim light, a circular space crammed with human figures, tier upon tier: the hired applauders and the public.

The popular movements, political clubs and solemn demonstrations of 1848 also provided Mr. G. with a series of excellently pictorial compositions, most of which were reproduced by *The Illustrated London News*. A few years ago, after a sojourn in Spain, which his genius found most fruitful, he put together a similar album, of which I have only seen fragments. The carelessness with which he lends or gives away his drawings has often caused irreparable losses.

VIII

THE MILITARY MAN

To define once again the type of subject preferred by our artist, I shall say that what he loves best is *the ceremonial life*, as it is to be seen in the capitals of the civilised world, in the ritual of the life of soldiering, the life of elegance and the life of courtship. Wherever flow those deep and impetuous desires, those Orinocos of the human heart—war, love and gaming; wherever we see the festivities and fictions that express these three great elements of happiness and misfortune, our observer is always at his post.

But his most marked predilection is for soldiering and the soldier; and I think that this is not only because of the virtues and qualities that are necessarily transmitted from the fighting man's soul to his face and bearing, but also because of the glaring finery in which the profession is attired. M. Paul de Molènes has written some charming and sensible pages concerning soldiers' preoccupation with their outward appearance and the moral significance of the glittering costumes in which all governments delight to array their troops. Mr. G. would willingly subscribe to all that M. de Molènes has written on this subject.

I have already spoken of the idiocy of supposing that beauty is confined to any particular period, and have remarked that every century has had, so to speak, its own personal attractiveness. The same remark can be applied to the professions: each of them derives the beauty of its outward show from the moral laws to which it is subject. In some this beauty will be characterised by energy; in others it will bear the obvious signs of leisure. It is a sort of stamp of quality, a seal of destiny.

The military man, in general, has his own beauty, just as the dandy and the courtesan have theirs, although in essentially different styles. (I shall readily be excused for not concerning myself here with trades in which monotonous and violent labour deforms the muscles and stamps the face with the mark of servitude).

Accustomed as he is to tactical surprises, the military man is not easily astonished. The especial mark of beauty in his case, therefore, will be a martial phlegm—a singular mixture of serenity and audacity; a beauty arising from the need to be prepared to die at any moment.

But another mark of the ideal soldier must necessarily be a great simplicity; for since they live communally, like monks or schoolboys, and are accustomed to unload the cares of daily life on to the shoulders of an abstract paternal authority, soldiers are in many ways as simple as children; and, once their duty has been accomplished, they are like children in being easily amused or easily led into violent diversions.

I think that I am not exaggerating when I say that all these general moral reflections arise of themselves from a study of Mr. G.'s drawings and water-colours. Every military type is represented in them, and all are portrayed with a sort of gleeful enthusiasm: the elderly infantry officer, grave and gloomy, wearying his horse with his obesity; the handsome staff-officer, with his pinched waist and swaggering shoulders, who boldly leans over armchairs where ladies are sitting, and, when seen from the rear, reminds one of some very slim and elegant insect; the light infantryman or skirmisher, whose bearing betrays exceeding audacity and independence, as well as something resembling a more lively sense of personal responsibility; the agile, free-and-easy carriage of the light cavalryman; the vaguely professional and academic appearance of members of auxiliary corps such as those of artillery and engineering (an appearance which is often enhanced by the unwarriorlike wearing of a pair of spectacles)—not one of these models, and not one of their shades of significance, has been omitted. All are summed up and defined with the same love and wit.

I have one of Mr. G.'s military compositions before me as I write. Its general appearance is nothing less than heroic. It shows the head of a column of infantry. Perhaps these men are returning from Italy and have made a halt on one of the boulevards, amidst the applause of the multitude; perhaps they have finished a long spell in Lombardy—I do not know. What is visibly and completely obvious is the firm, bold character, even under peaceful conditions, of all these faces tanned by sun, rain and wind.

Here one can well see the uniformity of expression that is created by a shared obedience and endurance; the submissive air of courage tested by long hardships. The trousers folded back and thrust into the gaiters; the hooded capes, dull with dust and vaguely discoloured—the whole of these troops' gear and equipment, in short—have acquired the ineffaceable stamp of beings who have come home from far away, and have had strange adventures. All these men seem to be more solidly based upon their own loins, to stand more squarely on their feet and to have more self-assurance than is possible for other men. If Charlet, who was always seeking for beauty of this kind, and so often found it, had seen this drawing, he would have been most deeply struck by it.

IX

THE DANDY

The man of wealth and leisure, who, even though weary of it, has no other occupation than the pursuit of pleasure; the man brought up in luxury and accustomed since his youth to the obedience of other men; the man, in short, who has no other profession but that of elegance, will always have a distinctive appearance, one that sets him utterly apart.

Dandyism is an institution as strange and obscure as the duel. It is very ancient, for Caesar, Catilina and Alcibiades were amongst its most brilliant representatives; and it is very widespread, for Chateaubriand has found it in the forests and on the lake-shores of the New World.

Dandyism, an institution above laws, has laws to which all its representatives—whatever extravagance or independence of character they may otherwise permit themselves—are strictly subject.

The English novelists, more than any others, have cultivated the novel of "high life"; and French authors, such as M. de Custine, who specialise in love stories, have always been careful, and very wisely so, to endow their characters with fortunes vast enough to enable them to pay without hesitation for all their fancies. These characters are therefore free from the need to follow any profession. They have no other purpose than to cultivate the idea of the beautiful in their own persons; to satisfy their desires, and to feel and think.

They therefore possess, *ad libitum* and in huge measure, the time and money without which fancy is reduced to a day-dream scarcely translatable into action. It is, unfortunately, quite true that without leisure and money love can be nothing but a plebeian orgy or the fulfilment of a conjugal duty. Instead of being a burning or fantastical caprice, it becomes a loathsome *utility*.

My reason for speaking of love in connection with dandyism is that love is the natural occupation of the leisured; but the dandy does not make love his special aim. Similarly, my reason for mentioning money is that money is indispensable to people who make a cult of their desires; but the dandy does not wish to have money for its own sake; he would be content to be allowed to live indefinitely on credit; he leaves the coarse desire for money to baser mortals.

Dandyism is not even, as many unthinking people seem to suppose, an immoderate interest in personal appearance and material elegance. For the true dandy these things are only a symbol of the aristocratic superiority of his personality. In his eyes, therefore, which seek, above all, distinction, the perfection of personal appearance consists in complete simplicity—this being, in fact, the best means of achieving distinction.

What, then, is this ruling passion that has turned into

a creed and created its own skilled tyrants? What is this unwritten constitution that has created so haughty a caste? It is, above all, a burning need to acquire originality, within the apparent bounds of convention. It is a sort of cult of oneself, which can dispense even with what are commonly called illusions. It is the delight in causing astonishment, and the proud satisfaction of never oneself being astonished. A dandy may be indifferent, or he may be unhappy; but in the latter case he will smile like the Spartan under the teeth of the fox.

It will be seen that, in certain aspects, dandyism borders on spirituality and stoicism. But a dandy can never indulge in anything vulgar. If he committed a crime, he would perhaps not be too upset about it; but if this crime had some trivial cause, his disgrace would be irreparable.

The reader should not be scandalised by this serious devotion to the frivolous. He should remember that there is a greatness in all follies, a strength in all extravagance. What a strange spiritual cult! For those who are at once its priests and victims, all the complicated material conditions to which they submit themselves—from the impeccable care of the person to the most dangerous forms of sport— are simply a gymnastic exercise designed to fortify the will and discipline the soul.

Indeed, I was not far wrong in regarding dandyism as a sort of religion. The most rigorous monastic order, or the absolute rule of the Old Man of the Mountain, who commanded his intoxicated disciples to kill themselves, was not more despotic, nor obtained stricter obedience, than this creed of elegance and originality. It, too, imposes on its ambitious yet humble devotees—men, often, of mettle, passion, courage and contained energy—the terrible formula: *Perinde ac cadaver!*

Whether the name they win for themselves be Corinthians, swells, bucks, lions or dandies, their origin is the same.

They all have the same characteristics of opposition and revolt. They all represent the best element in human pride—that need, which nowadays is too uncommon, to combat and destroy triviality. This is what gives the dandy his haughty attitude, the attitude of a caste whose very reserve is a provocation.

Dandyism arises especially in periods of transition, when democracy is not yet all-powerful and aristocracy is only partially tottering or brought low. In the disturbance of such periods a certain number of men, detached from their own class, disappointed and disorientated, but still rich in native energy, may form a project of founding a new sort of aristocracy, which will be all the more difficult to break because it will be based on the most precious and indestructible of human powers—on those celestial gifts that neither toil nor money can bestow.

Dandyism is the last gleam of heroism in times of decadence. The fact that a type of dandy was discovered by a traveller in North America does not invalidate this statement; for there is nothing to prevent us from supposing that what we call the "savage" tribes are the debris of great vanished civilisations. Dandyism is a setting sun. Like the great sinking star, it is superb, cold and melancholy.

But alas! the rising tide of democracy, overwhelming and levelling everything, is day by day drowning these last champions of human pride, washing the waves of oblivion over the traces of these prodigious myrmidons. In France the dandy is becoming more and more rare; although amongst our English neighbours the social conditions and the constitution (that true constitution, which expresses itself in daily life) will for a long time yet leave a place for the heirs of Sheridan, Brummell and Byron—if, that is to say, worthy heirs present themselves.

All this may have seemed to the reader a digression, but in fact it is not one. The reflections and moralising fancies provoked by an artist's work are often the best introduction to them that a critic can offer. All the suggestions that an artist makes to us are the offspring of a begetting idea; and by describing each of these suggestions severally, one may convey a notion of the idea itself.

Need I say that, when Mr. G. sets one of his dandies down on paper, he always gives him his historical character—his legendary character, I would venture to say, were it not that we are here concerned with matters of the present time, and with matters that are commonly regarded as objects of mirth? You can find everything there: that alertness of bearing; that certainty of behaviour; that simplicity in the air of supremacy; that manner of wearing a coat or managing a horse; those attitudes always serene but indicative of strength—all the things that cause us to reflect, when our eye lights upon one of those privileged beings in whom the gracious and the formidable are so mysteriously compounded: " There goes what may be a rich man, but is certainly a resting Hercules!"

The characteristic beauty of the dandy consists, above all, in his air of reserve, which in turn, arises from his unshakeable resolve not to feel any emotion. It might be likened to a hidden fire whose presence can be guessed at; a fire that could blaze up, but does not wish to do so. This is what is so perfectly expressed in Mr. G.'s pictures.

X

WOMAN

The Being who for most men is the source of the most vivid and also (let it be said to the shame of the sensual pleasures of philosophy) the most lasting delights; the Being towards whom, or for whose benefit, all the efforts of most men are directed; that Being who is as terrible and incommunicable as God (but with this difference, that the Infinite does not communicate because it would blind and overwhelm the Finite, whereas the Being of whom we speak is perhaps incomprehensible only because she has nothing to communicate); that Being in whom Joseph de Maistre saw "a beautiful animal" whose charms lent gaiety and facility to the serious game of politics; that Being for whom, and through whom, fortunes are made and unmade; for whom, but especially *through whom*, artists and poets create their finest jewels; the source of the most enervating pleasures and the most fruitful griefs:—Woman, in a word, is not, either for the artist, in general, or for Mr. G. in particular, merely the feminine gender of man.

She is rather a divinity, a star that presides over all the parturitions of the male brain. She is a reflection of all the charms of nature concentrated in an individual. She is the focus of the most vivid admiration and interest that the picture of life has to offer the beholder. She is a sort of idol—stupid, maybe, but dazzling—an enchantress holding all human wills and destinies suspended in her glance.

She is not, I say, an animal whose limbs, when correctly put together, provide a perfect example of harmony. She is not even a typefaction of pure beauty, such as a sculptor might dream of in his austerest meditations. No, none of that would suffice to explain the mysterious and complex enchantment. This is something not to be found in Winckelmann or Raphael; and I am convinced that Mr. G., despite the great breadth of his intelligence (I hope I am not insulting him), would turn from any piece of antique statuary rather than lose a chance of gazing at a portrait by Reynolds or Lawrence.

All that adorns a woman, all that serves to illuminate her beauty, is a part of herself; and these artists who have especially applied themselves to the study of this enigmatic

Being are as passionately obsessed with all the appur-
tenances of the *mundus muliebris* as with the person of
Woman herself.

Woman is clearly a ray of light, a look, an invitation to
happiness, sometimes a watchword; but especially she is a
general harmony, not only in her bearing and the movement
of her limbs, but also in the muslins, the gauzes and the great,
iridescent clouds of the stuffs that envelop her, and are, so to
speak, the attributes or the pedestal of her divinity; in the
metals and minerals that twine around her neck and arms,
adding their sparkles to the fire of her glances or softly
prattling at her ears.

What poet would dare, in depicting the delight caused by a
beauteous apparition, to distinguish between the woman and
her garb? Where is the man who, in street, theatre or public
park, has not taken an utterly disinterested pleasure in a
skilfully composed attire, and gone away with a mental
picture in which this latter is inseparably mingled with the
beauty of its owner—thus making of the woman and her
garb an indivisible whole?

This is the moment, it seems to me, to return to certain
questions, concerning fashion and personal adornment, on
which I only lightly touched at the beginning of this essay;
and a moment to take vengeance, on behalf of the art of
cultivating the personal appearance, for the stupid slanders
uttered against it by certain extremely dubious "nature-
lovers."

XI

IN PRAISE OF COSMETICS

There is a popular song which is so trivial and silly that
it can scarcely be quoted in an essay with some pretensions

to be serious, but which accurately interprets, in musical comedy style, the aesthetic views of unthinking people:

"Nature lends a charm to beauty."

One may presume that, had the 'poet' been able to write French, he would have written:

"Simplicity lends charm to beauty",

which gives this profound sentiment an entirely new meaning. An *absence* of something embellishes something that is present.

Most of the errors concerning beauty arise from the false moral concepts of the eighteenth century. At that time nature was taken as the foundation, source and type of all that could be good or beautiful. The denial of original sin had not a little to do with the general blindness of this period.

If, however, we consent to pay heed simply to the visible facts—to the experience of all the ages and to the Police Court Gazette—we shall see that nature teaches us nothing, or almost nothing. It *compels* man to sleep, drink and eat, and to secure himself, to the best of his ability, against surrounding dangers. It is nature, too, that drives man to kill his neighbour, to eat him, to confiscate his goods and to torture him; for, as soon as we quit the field of natural necessities and desires for that of luxuries and pleasures, we see that nature can be a counseller only of crime. It is this so-infallible nature, too, that has created parricide and cannibalism, as well as a thousand other abominations that modesty and delicacy forbid us to name. On the other hand, it is philosophy (a right philosophy, I mean) and religion that bid us cherish the poor and sick amongst our kinsmen. Nature, which is simply the voice of our self-interest, bids us knock them on the head.

Carefully survey and analyse everything that is natural, all the actions and desires of the pure natural man, and you will find nothing that is not horrible. Everything beautiful and noble is the result of reason and thought.

Crime, for which the human animal acquires a taste in his mother's belly, is of natural origin. Virtue, on the contrary, is *artificial* and supernatural—since at all times and in all nations it has taken gods and prophets to teach it to the human animal, and man by himself would have been powerless to discover it. Evil arises, of itself, *naturally* and by predestination. Good is always the product of a creative skill.

All that I have said of nature as an evil counseller in matters of morality, and of reason as a true redeemer and reformer, can be translated in terms of the beautiful. I am therefore inclined to regard personal adornment as one of the signs of the primitive nobility of the human soul. The races that our confused and perverted civilisation likes to look upon as savages—thereby showing a ridiculous conceit and fatuity—these races understand as well as a child does the exalted spirituality of the care of the person. The savage and the baby both bear witness, by their ingenuous love of brilliance, of motley plumage, iridescent stuffs and the superlative majesty of the creations of artifice, to their disdain of the real—thus unwittingly proving the absence of materialism in their souls.

Woe to him who, like Louis XV (who was the product not of a true civilisation, but of a relapse into barbarism) carries depravity to the point of enjoying "simple nature." *

Fashion should therefore be regarded as a symptom of that attachment to the ideal which is superimposed in the human brain upon all the coarse, terrestrial and foul accumulations of natural life; it should be regarded as a sublime deformity of nature, or rather as a continual and ever-renewed attempt to reform nature.

* It is known that, when Mme Dubarry wished not to receive the King, she was careful to wear rouge. This was a sufficient sign that her door was closed. Embellishment was her method of putting to flight this royal disciple of nature. *Author's footnote.*

The experience of our senses teaches us (although without telling us the reason) that all fashions are charming—that is to say, charming in relation to their circumstances; each fashion being a new, more or less successful, striving towards the beautiful; some sort of approximation to an ideal towards which the restless spirit of mankind is incessantly spurred.

If one wishes to appreciate fashions, however, one must not regard them as lifeless objects. One might as well admire the cast-offs that hang, as listless and inert as the skin of St. Bartholomew, on the racks of an old-clothes shop. They must be seen as vitalised and vivified by the lively women who wore them. Only thus can one understand their spirit and meaning. If, therefore, the statement: "All fashions are charming" disturbs you, as being too sweeping, you can avoid all possibility of misunderstanding by changing it to: "Every fashion had its own legitimate charm."

Woman is well within her rights, and is indeed performing a sort of duty, in studying to appear magical and supernatural. It is necessary that she should astonish and bewitch. Being an idol, she must be gilded to be adored. She must therefore borrow from all the arts the means of raising herself above nature, the better to subjugate hearts and stir souls. It matters very little that her tricks and artifices should be known to all, provided that their success is certain and their effect always irresistible.

Such considerations provide the artist-philosopher with a ready justification for all the practices employed by women of every period to lend substance and, so to speak, divinity to their fragile beauty.

An enumeration of these practices would be interminable. But to confine ourselves to what our contemporaries vulgarly call "the use of cosmetics", who can fail to see that the use of rice-powder (so stupidly anathematised by our candid philosophers) has the object and result of banishing from the complexion the blemishes which nature has outrageously sown there, and of creating an abstract unity in the texture and colour of the skin; and that this unity, like the unity produced by the sculptor's chisel, brings the human being directly nearer to the statue—in other words, to a being that is divine and superior? As for the lamp-black that outlines the eye, and the rouge that emphasises the upper part of the cheek, the planned result of these—although their use arises from the same principle, the need to transcend nature—is to satisfy an exactly opposite need. The red and the black represent life—a life surpassing and exceeding that of nature. That black frame around the eye makes the glance stranger and more penetrating; it makes the eye more distinctly resemble a window open on the infinite. That red blaze on the cheek further enhances the brightness of the eye, and lends a woman's lovely face the mysterious passion of a priestess.

This means, if I am rightly understood, that the face should not be painted with the vulgar and necessarily secret purpose of imitating the beauties of nature and setting up a rivalry with youth. In any case, it is well known that artifice cannot beautify ugliness, but can be a servant only to beauty. Who would dare assign to art the sterile task of imitating nature? Cosmetics should not seek to avoid detection; on the contrary, they should flaunt themselves, if not with ostentation then at least with a sort of frankness.

Readers whose heavy seriousness prevents them from seeking beauty in its most minute forms have my leave to laugh at these thoughts of mine, and accuse them of a puerile solemnity. I am not in the least affected by their strict judgment; I shall be content to appeal to true artists, as well as to those women who have received at birth a spark of that sacred flame with which they wish to illuminate their whole beings.

XII

WOMEN AND COURTESANS

Having taken on the task of seeking and revealing beauty in *modernity*, Mr. G. is fond of depicting women highly adorned and beautified by all the rites of artifice—to whatever order of society they may belong. (It may be noted that throughout his work, as in the swarm of living humanity, racial and class differences, under whatever mask of luxury, leap immediately to the spectator's eye).

Sometimes he depicts young women of the best society, bathed in the diffused glow of a place of entertainment, receiving and reflecting the light in their eyes, in their jewels and on their shoulders—as brilliant as portraits, set in their theatre-boxes as if in frames. Some are grave and serious, others fair-haired and languishing. Some flaunt, with aristocratic lack of concern, a precious throat; others candidly display a boyish bosom. They tap their teeth with their fans, their glances are vague or fixed; they are as theatrical and solemn as the drama or opera to which they are pretending to listen.

Sometimes he shows us smart families serenely strolling along the paths of public parks; the women leaning, with an air of placidity, on their husband's arms, whilst the men's air of solidity and satisfaction reveals the achievement of financial fortune and spiritual self-complacence. Here, instead of high distinction, we have a parade of substance. Skinny little girls with wide skirts, looking like little women in their style and gestures, play with skipping-ropes, trundle hoops or "go visiting" in the open air, in reproduction of the comedies played in their homes by their parents.

In other pictures, young actresses in unimportant theatres, slender, fragile, still adolescent beings who have risen from

c

lowly station and are proud at last to have emerged into the sun of the footlights, wear on their virginal and puny frames absurd travesties of costumes, which belong to no period and are their constant joy.

At the door of a café, leaning against the glass panes illumined from without and from within, swaggers one of those imbeciles whose elegance is created by their tailors and whose heads by their barbers. Beside him sits his mistress, her feet supported on the indispensable footstool—a comical creature who lacks almost nothing (and this almost nothing is almost everything; it is precisely what constitutes distinction) that could make her resemble a great lady. The whole orifice of her tiny mouth is filled, like the mouth of her handsome companion, with an outsize cigar. These two beings do not think. Can one be quite sure that they even see? Unless, perhaps, Narcissuses of imbecility, they are gazing on the crowd as on a stream that gives them back their own image. The fact is that they exist much more for the pleasure of the observer than for their own.

And here, displaying their galleries full of light and movement, are all the Valentino's, Casino's and Prado's (formerly Tivoli's, Idalia's, Follies and Paphoses), those bear-gardens where the exuberance of idle youth is given full rein. Women who have exaggerated contemporary fashion, until its charm and purpose are destroyed, ostentatiously sweep the parquet floors with the trains of their gowns and the ends of their shawls. They come and go, pass and repass, their eyes wide and astonished like the eyes of animals; they have an air of seeing nothing, but they scrutinise everything.

Against backgrounds of the illumination of hell or of the aurora borealis, backgrounds red, orange, sulphur-yellow or rose-pink (a colour that reveals an idea of ecstasy in frivolity) or sometimes violet (the preferred colour of canonesses, that of a fire dying out behind a curtain of heavenly azure)—against these magic back-grounds, with their diverse imitations of Bengal fire, arises the varied image of intruding Beauty; here majestic, there light-hearted; sometimes slender, or even scrawny, sometimes Cyclopean; sometimes small and sparkling, sometimes heavy and monumental. Now she has invented a barbarous, provocative elegance; now she aims, with greater or less success, at the simplicity affected by persons above her station. She advances, glides, dances, trundles beneath her load of embroidered petticoats which serve her at once as a pedestal and as a balancing-pole. She darts glances from beneath her hat, like a portrait in its frame. She well represents the element of savagery in civilisation. She has the beauty lent her by Evil—always utterly devoid of anything spiritual, but sometimes tinged with a fatigue that apes melancholy. She fixes her gaze on the horizon, like a beast of prey—with the same bewilderment, the same indolent curiosity, and sometimes also with the same alertness. A Bohemian straying on the fringes of a normal society, the triviality of her life—a life of trickery and combat—shines inexorably through her enveloping apparatus. To her can justly be applied the words of Bruyère, that inimitable master: "Some women have an artificial grandeur which derives from the movement of the eyes, the carriage of the head, a manner of walking, and has no further significance."

What can be said of the courtesan can also be said, with reservations, of the actress; for the latter, too, is a manufactured confection and a thing of public pleasure. But where the actress is concerned, the conquest and the booty are more noble, more spiritual. Her business is to win general favour not only by her physical beauty, but also by talents of the rarest order. If on one side the actress is akin to the courtesan, on the other side she is akin to the poet. We must remember that, apart from any natural beauty and even from any artificial beauty, all human creatures are stamped with the idiom of their trade—a characteristic that can physically express itself in ugliness, but also in a sort of beauty of the profession.

In this huge gallery of life as it is lived in London or Paris we meet the various types of the woman who has gone astray, of the woman in revolt against society, at all her stages.

First we see the toast of the town, in the flower of her beauty, aspiring to the airs of a patrician, proud both of her youth and of her luxury, into which latter she puts all her gifts and all her soul. Delicately she turns up, between two fingers, a broad panel of the satin, silk, or velvet that floats around her, and thrusts forward a pointed foot, whose over-ornamented shoe would alone suffice to betray what she is, even without the somewhat vivid emphasis of her whole attire.

Descending the ladder, we come to the female slaves confined in those low retreats that are often decorated to resemble cafés; unfortunate beings under the most avaricious tutelage, who possess nothing of their own, not even the eccentric rig-outs that serve as a condiment to their beauty.

Some of these latter—specimens of an innocent and monstrous fatuity—display in their features and boldly direct glances an obvious pleasure in existence ("Why?" one could well ask.) Sometimes they unintentionally fall into attitudes of an audacity and nobility that would enchant the most sensitive sculptor—if only the sculptor of today had the courage and intelligence to find nobility everywhere, even in the mire. At other times they are shown prostrate in desperate attitudes of boredom, in the indolent stupors of café existence, filled with a masculine cynicism, smoking cigarettes to kill time with the resignation of oriental fatalism; ostentatiously sprawling on divans, with skirt tucked up before and behind in a double fan, or balanced on stools or chairs: heavy, gloomy, stupid, garish, their eyes glazed by brandy and their foreheads bulging with petulance.

We have descended to the bottom of the spiral, to the femina simplex of Latin satire. Sometimes we see depicted, amidst an atmosphere in which alcohol and tobacco have mingled their reeks, the inflamed emaciation of phthisis, or the curves of adiposity, that hideous health of the idle. A foggy and gilded chaos, without a trace of the chastities of indigence, is filled with the gesticulations and writhings of macabre nymphs or living dolls from whose infantile cheeks gleams a sinister brightness. Behind a counter laden with bottles of liquor lounges a bulky Megaera, her head swathed in a dirty scarf that throws on the wall a satanically pointed shadow, provoking the reflection that everything dedicated to Evil is condemned to wear horns.

I can assure you, it is not to make the reader feel comfortable, any more than to scandalise him, that I have held such pictures before his eyes. To do either would be to fail in respect towards him. What gives these pictures their great and consecrated worth is the multitude of reflections, mostly severe and sombre, to which they give rise. But if, by chance, any ill-advised person were to seek in these compositions of Mr. G., which can be found almost anywhere, an opportunity of satisfying an unwholesome curiosity, I must charitably warn him that he will find nothing in them to excite a morbid imagination. He will find nothing but the inevitable spectacle of vice—the glower of the demon at ambush in the darkness, or Messalina's shoulder glistening in the gaslight; nothing but pure art—that is to say, the peculiar beauty of Evil, the beauty of the horrible. In fact, let me repeat it in passing, the general feeling inspired by all this Gomorrah is more saddening than entertaining. What gives these pictures their special beauty is the richness of their moral content. They are highly suggestive—but of cruel and bitter things, to which my pen, although accustomed to struggle with the description of plastic forms, has perhaps been unable to do sufficient justice.

XIII

CARRIAGES

So they extend, interrupted by countless side-passages, these long galleries of "high life" and "low life." Let us emigrate for a brief while to a world which, though it may not be pure, is at least more refined. Let us breathe in scents that may not be more wholesome, but are at least more delicate.

I have already said that Mr. G.'s brush, like that of Mr. Eugène Lami, is marvellously adept at the depiction of the rites of dandyism and the elegance of the world of female fashion. He is familiar with the attitudes of the rich. By a light stroke of the pen, and with a confidence that is never at a loss, he can depict that assurance of look, gesture and posture which, amongst privileged beings, is the result of a monotony of good fortune.

The series of sketches that we shall next consider reproduces a thousand aspects of sport, racing, hunting, drives in the park—proud "ladies" and slender "misses" expertly directing steeds of an admirable purity of line, steeds as dainty, brilliant and capricious as their mistresses. For Mr. G. not only knows the horse in general, but also has a happy gift for expressing the individual beauties of horses.

Sometimes we see static scenes—encampments, so to speak, of several carriages at a time. Emerging from these and perched on cushions, chairs or the roofs of the carriages themselves, slim young men and women accoutred in the eccentric costumes permitted by the season are watching some ceremony of the turf, which is proceeding in the distance. Sometimes we see a horseman gracefully galloping beside an open barouche; the curvettings of his horse give the impression that the animal, too, is in its own fashion paying its respects. The carriage is rapidly proceeding down an avenue zebra-striped with light and shade, carrying a bevy of beauties reclining indolently, as if in a cockle-shell. They vaguely listen to the gallantries assailing their ears, and idly bathe in the breeze of the drive.

Their furs or muslins rise to their chins, and surge like a wave through the carriage door. The servants are stiff and perpendicular, motionless and all alike—always the same unrelieved and monotonous effigies of servitude; their characteristic feature is to have no characteristic feature.

In the background the park is green or russet, dusty or dark, according to the season and time of day. Its sheltered spots are full of autumn mists, blue shadows, yellow brightness, roseate glows or thin shafts of light that cut like swords through the gloom.

If Mr. G.'s countless water-colours of the war in the East had not already demonstrated his power as a painter of landscape, these sketches would surely suffice to do so. But here, in place of the war-torn terrain of the Crimea or the theatrical shores of the Bosphorus, we find the familiar and intimate landscapes that are the decorative setting of a great city. Here the light creates effects that no truly romantic artist can disdain.

Another of Mr. G.'s gifts which can well be mentioned here is his remarkable knowledge of harnesses and carriages. Mr. G. draws and paints a carriage—all kinds of carriages— with the care and ease that a consummate painter of naval subjects would give to his paintings of every sort of ship. All his coachwork is perfectly correct; everything is in its proper place, and there is nothing there that shouldn't be there. Whatever the posture into which it may be thrown, whatever the gait at which it may be travelling, a carriage, like a ship, is lent by its movement a mysterious and complex grace which it is very difficult to note down in shorthand.

The pleasure that the artist's eye obtains is derived, so it seems, from the series of geometrical figures that the object in question—of itself so complicated, whether ship or coach—successively and rapidly creates in space.

We can wager with certainty that within not many years Mr. G.'s sketches will have become valuable records of civilised life. His work will be sought after by students as eagerly as that of men like Debucourt, Moreau, Saint-Aubin, Carle Vernet, Lami, Devéria, Gavarni or any other of those exquisite artists who, for all that they painted only the familiar and the pretty, are none the less, in their own fashion, serious historians.

Several of these men have even made too great a sacrifice to prettiness, and have sometimes introduced into their compositions a classical style that is foreign to the subject. Several of them have wilfully rounded off the corners and smoothed out the rough edges of life, thus dulling its lightning-brilliance. Mr. G., less adroit than these, retains a deep merit all his own. He has deliberately performed a task that artists disdain, and which it was especially left for a man of the world to perform. He has sought, in the ephemeral and fleeting beauty of present-day life, the stamp of what, by the reader's leave, we have called "modernity." Often strange, violent and extravagant, he has known how to concentrate in his sketches the bitter or heady flavour of the wine of life.

THE POEM OF HASHISH

THE POEM OF HASHISH

(from *Paradise by Artifice*)

I

THE LONGING FOR THE INFINITE

Any man skilled in the study of his own nature, and able to retain the impression that life has made upon him—any man capable, as Hoffmann was, of constructing his own spiritual barometer—has now and then noticed, from the Observatory of his intellect, various seasons of fine weather, daytimes of happiness, minutes of delight.

There are days when a man wakes up full of a young, vigorous inspiration. With the dust of sleep scarcely out of his eyes, the material world offers him, in bold relief, an amazing clearness of outline and wealth of colour. The world of the spirit opens up huge perspectives, full of new glimpses. A man granted this blessed privilege, which unfortunately is rare and fleeting, feels himself more creative and more moral—a nobler being, in short.

But the oddest thing about this uncommon state of the soul and senses—a state that I can describe without exaggeration as paradisal, if I compare it with the heavy darkness of communal and day-to-day existence—is that it is due to no easily visible or definable cause.

Is it the result of well-cared-for health and a sensible diet? This is the first explanation that occurs to the mind; but we are compelled to recognise that often this wonder—this miracle, so to speak—comes into existence as if produced by a superior and invisible force, external to the man himself, and after a period in which he has actually been abusing his physical faculties.

Shall we say, then, that it is the reward of assiduous prayer and spiritual fervency? It is certainly true that a constant uplifting of desire, a taut striving of the soul towards heaven, would be the most suitable regimen for the creation of this brilliant and glorious spiritual health. But what absurd law permits it sometimes to appear after shameful orgies of the imagination—or after a sophisticated and deliberate abuse of the mental powers, an abuse that bears the same relation to the proper and reasonable use of these as a contortionist's tricks do to healthy gymnastics? That is why I prefer to regard this abnormal state of the mind as a true "gift of grace"; as a magic mirror in which the recipient is invited to see himself in all his beauty—that is to say, as he should and could be; as a sort of angelic bidding, a fall-in-on-parade couched in complimentary terms. It is just so that a certain religious school, which has representatives in England and America, regards supernatural phenomena such as ghostly apparitions, hauntings, etc., as manifestations of the Divine Will intent on reawakening in man's spirit the memory of invisible realities.

It may be remarked that this strange and delightful state, in which all the forces are in equilibrium, so that the imagination, although wondrously powerful, does not drag the moral sense after it into perilous adventures, nor is the exquisite sensibility tortured by sick nerves—this marvellous state, as I was saying, has no precursory symptoms. It is as unexpected as a phantom. It is a kind of haunting visitation, but an intermittent one, from which we should gain, if we were wise, the certainty of a better existence, and the hope of attaining it by a daily exercise of our will.

This mental acumen, this inspiration of the soul and senses, must always have seemed to mankind the chief of blessings. That is why man has always sought—in all

climes and at all times, and without disturbing himself with
the thought that he was breaking the laws of his nation—
to find in physical science, in pharmacy, in the grossest
liquors or the subtlest perfumes, the means to escape, if
only for a few hours, from his habitation in the mire, and,
as the author of '*Lazare*' puts it, "to capture Paradise at
a stroke".

How sad that man's vices, however horrible we may
conceive them to be, themselves contain the proof (be it
only in their infinite ramifications!) of his longing for the
Infinite.

The trouble is that this longing often goes astray. The
common proverb: "All roads lead to Rome" might be
metaphorically interpreted to apply in the sphere of morals.
Everything leads to reward or punishment—two forms of
eternity. The human spirit overflows with passion; it has
"enough and to spare" of it to use another trivial
expression. But this unfortunate spirit, whose natural
depravity is as great as its sudden and almost paradoxical
inclinations towards charity and the most arduous virtues,
is rich in paradoxes that allow it to employ this overflowing
surplus of passion in the service of Evil.

The spirit never believes that it is selling itself wholesale.
It forgets, in its infatuation, that it is playing against an
opponent subtler and stronger than itself; and that, if one
lets the Spirit of Evil but grasp a hair of one's head, he is not
slow to carry off the head itself.

This visible lord of visible nature (man, I mean) has
therefore sought to construct Paradise from drugs or
fermented drinks—like a maniac using stage-sets, painted
on canvas and mounted on frames, as a substitute for real
furniture and gardens. In this corruption of the sense of the
Infinite lies, in my view, the reason for all culpable excess:
from the solitary and concentrated drunkenness of the
writer who has been forced to seek relief from physical pain

in opium, and, having thus found a source of unwholesome pleasures, has gradually made of it his only means of physical refreshment, and the sun of his spiritual life—to the most squalid tipsiness of some suburban drinker ridiculously sprawling, with his brain alight with fire and glory in the filth of the street.

Amongst the drugs that best serve to create what I call "the artificial Ideal"—if we leave aside liquors that quickly drive a man into physical furore and deliver a knock-out blow to the strength of his spirit, or inhalants whose excessive use, whilst making a man's imagination more subtle, gradually exhausts his physical powers—apart from these, the two most effective agents, and those whose employment is most convenient and most ready to hand, are hashish and opium. The purpose of this study is to analyse the mysterious effects and morbid delights that these drugs can engender; the inevitable retribution resulting from their prolonged use; and, lastly, the essential immorality implicit in this pursuit of a false ideal.

The definitive work on opium has already been written, and in so brilliant a fashion, at once poetic and medically sound, that I would not dare to add anything to it. I shall therefore confine myself to offering, in another article, an analysis of this incomparable work, which has never been translated into French in its entirety. The author, a famous writer, of powerful and exquisite imagination, who is today living in silent retirement, has dared, with tragic candour, to give a full account of the delights and tortures that, in his time, he has discovered in opium; and the most dramatic part of his book is that in which he speaks of the superhuman efforts of will that he had to put forth in order to escape the doom to which he had recklessly condemned himself.

Today I shall speak only of hashish. My account of it will be based on a great quantity of detailed information, extracts from written or verbal statements by intelligent men who were for a long time addicts. I shall simply blend these various documents into a sort of monograph, selecting a single soul—one that, for choice, is easy to explain and define—as a typical victim of experiences of this nature.

II

WHAT IS HASHISH?

The tales of Marco Polo—which it is a mistake to deride like those of some other ancient travellers—have been verified by scholars, and merit our belief. I shall not repeat his story of how the Old Man of the Mountain used to intoxicate his young disciples with hashish (whence the word "Hashishin" or "Assassins") and then shut them up in a garden full of delights, with the object of giving them a foretaste of Paradise, and thus exacting from them, in exchange, a passive and unthinking obedience. On the subject of the secret society of the Hashishin the reader may consult the book by M. de Hammer, and the study by M. Sylvestre de Sacy contained in Volume XVI of the *Studies by the Academy of Inscriptions and Belles Letters'*; also concerning the etymology of the word "assassin", the latter gentleman's letter to the editor of the *Moniteur* published in issue No. 359 of the year 1809.

Herodotus reports that the Scythians used to collect piles of hemp-seed, on which they threw red-hot stones. In this way they got a sort of steam-bath, more deliciously perfumed than that of any Greek hot-room, and the pleasure was so keen that it moved them to shouts of joy.

Hashish does, in fact, come to us from the East. The stimulating properties of hemp were well known in ancient Egypt, and its use is very widespread, under different names, in India, Algeria and Arabia Felix. But we also have in our own midst curious examples of the intoxication caused by herbal fumes. it is known that children, after romping and rolling on heaps of mown lucern, often undergo odd spells of dizziness, and it is also known that during the hemp harvest the male and female reapers have similar experiences. The harvest seems to give off a miasma that malignantly disturbs their brains. The reaper's head is filled with whirling eddies, or sometimes heavy with dreamy fancies. At certain moments the limbs grow weak and refuse to function. We have heard of fairly frequent cases of somnambulism amongst Russian peasants, caused, it is said, by the use of hemp-seed oil in their cooking. Who is not familiar with the extravagant behaviour of chickens that have eaten hemp, or the mettlesome eagerness of peasant's horses at fairs and on saints' days, when their masters have prepared them for a steeplechase with a dose of hemp-seed, sometimes mixed with wine?

Nevertheless, French hemp is unsuitable for conversion into hashish—or at least, as frequent experience has shown, it is incapable of producing a drug of equal power.

Hashish, or Indian hemp, *cannabis indica*, is a plant of the nettle tribe, similar in all respects, except that it grows less high, to the hemp of our climes. It has most extraordinary properties of intoxication, which for several years have been in France an object of study by scientists and by people of good society. The esteem in which it is held varies with its place of origin: the hemp of Bengal is that most valued by connoisseurs; but those of Egypt, Constantinople, Persia, and Algeria possess the same properties, only in lesser degree.

The "herb" (for this is the meaning of the word "hashish"—the "herb" par excellence—as if the Arabs had wished to sum up in a single word the source of all non-physical pleasures) bears different names according to its composition and the mode of preparation it has undergone in the country where it was harvested: in India, "bhang"; in Africa, "teriaki"; in Algeria and Arabia Felix, "madjound", etc. The season of year at which it is gathered makes a big difference: it is when the plant is in flower that it possesses the greatest potency. Consequently, only its flowery tops are used in the various preparations that I shall now briefly describe.

The "rich extract" of hashish, as prepared by the Arabs, is obtained by cooking the tops of the plant, while still fresh, in butter with a little water. When all humidity has evaporated, the residue is passed through a sieve. Thus is obtained a preparation looking like a yellow-greenish hair-oil and retaining a disagreeable odour of hashish and rancid butter. In this form it is taken in little pellets of two to four grammes; but, because of its revolting smell, which continually grows stronger, the Arabs encase the rich extract in sweetmeats.

The most common of these sweetmeats, the "dawamesk", is a mixture of rich extract, sugar and various flavourings, such as vanilla, cinnamon, pistachio, almond and musk. Sometimes even a little cantharides is added, with a purpose quite at variance from the normal purposes of hashish.

In this form, hashish is completely rid of its disagreeable quality, and can be taken in doses of fifteen, twenty or thirty grammes, either wrapped in a wafer or immersed in a cup of coffee.

The object of experiments by Messrs. Smith, Gastinel and Decourtive was to discover the active principle of hashish. Despite their efforts, its chemical components and their inter-reaction are as yet little known; but its properties are generally ascribed to a resinous substance that is present in fairly substantial quantity—in a proportion of about ten per cent. To obtain this resin, the plant is dried, ground to a coarse powder and washed several times in alcohol, which is then distilled in order to draw off a part of it. The substance is then dried off until it has the consistency of an extract. This extract is treated with water, which dissolves the gummy foreign bodies, and the residue is the pure resin.

This product is soft in texture, of a dark-green colour, and possesses to a high degree the characteristic odour of hashish. Five, ten or fifteen hundredths of a gramme are enough to produce surprising effects.

Another form of the drug, hashishin, can be taken in chocolate-coated pastilles or little ginger-flavoured pills. It produces, like the dawamesk or like rich extract, effects of varying intensity and character, according to the temperament and nervous susceptibility of the taker. Still better, the result varies in one and the same individual: sometimes it will be an immoderate and irresistible gaiety, sometimes a sensation of well-being and plenitude of life; at other times a dubious and dream-shot half-slumber. Certain phenomena, however, are fairly constant, especially amongst people of similar temperament and education. There is a sort of unity within variety—which is the reason why I shall not have too much difficulty in compiling the monograph, of which I was just now speaking, on this particular form of intoxication.

In Constantinople, in Algeria, and even in France, some people smoke hashish mixed with tobacco; but in their cases the phenomena I mentioned occur only in a very mild and, so to speak, sluggish form. I have heard it said that recently it has been found possible, by a process of distillation, to extract from hashish an essential oil that appears to have a much more active character than any preparation known hitherto. But this product has not been sufficiently investigated to enable me to describe its results with any certainty.

Is it hardly necessary to add that tea, coffee and spirituous liquors are all powerful adjuvants and accelerate, in greater or less degree, the flowering of this mysterious intoxication.

III

THE SERAPHIC THEATRE

"What does one experience? What does one see? Wonderful things, eh? Amazing sights? Is it very beautiful? Very terrible? Very dangerous?"

Such are the questions put, with a mixture of curiosity and fear, by the ignorant to the initiated. The questioners seem to have a childish impatience for knowledge, such as might be felt by somebody who has never left his fireside, on meeting a man returning from distant and unknown lands. They think of the intoxication caused by hashish as a land of miracles, a huge conjuror's theatre where everything is marvellous and unexpected.

This is an ill-informed notion, a complete misunderstanding. Since, for the common run of readers and questioners, the word hashish conveys an idea of strange, topsy-turvy worlds, an expectation of miraculous dreams (a more accurate word would be hallucinations—which, in any case, are less frequent than is generally supposed), I shall at once point out an important difference between the effects of hashish and the phenomena of sleep.

In sleep, that nightly journey of adventure, there positively is something miraculous; although the miracle's mystery has been staled by its punctual regularity. Men's dreams are of two kinds. Those of the first kind are full of his ordinary life, his preoccupations, desires and faults, mingled in a more or less bizarre fashion with things seen during the day that have indiscriminately attached themselves to the huge canvas of his memory. This is the natural dream—the man himself.

But the other kind of dream! The absurd, unpredictable dream, with no relation to or connection with the character,

life or passions of the dreamer. This, which I shall call the
"hieroglyphic" dream, obviously represents the supernatural
side of life; and it is just because of its absurdity that the
ancients regarded it as divine. Since it cannot be explained
as a product of natural causes, they attributed it to a
cause external to mankind; and even today, and apart from
the oneiromancers, there is a school of philosophy that sees
in dreams of this sort sometimes a reproach and sometimes a
counsel; a symbolic moral picture, that is to say, engendered
actually in the mind of the sleeping person. It is a dictionary
that requires study for its comprehension, a language to
which wise men can obtain the key.

The intoxication of hashish is utterly different. It will
not bring us beyond the bounds of the natural dream. It is
true that throughout its whole period the intoxication will
be in the nature of a vast dream—by reason of the intensity
of its colours and its rapid flow of mental images; but it will
always retain the private tonality of the individual. The
man wanted the dream, now the dream will govern the man;
but this dream will certainly be the son of its father. The
sluggard has contrived artificially to introduce the supernatural into his life and thoughts; but he remains, despite
the adventitious force of his sensations, merely the same
man increased, the same number raised to a very high
power. He is subjugated—but, unfortunately for him, only
by himself; in other words, by that part of himself that was
already previously dominant. *He wished to ape the angel, he
has become an animal;* and for a brief while the latter is very
powerful—if power is the correct word for an excessive
sensibility—because it is subject to no restraining or directing government.

It is right then, that sophisticated persons, and also
ignorant persons who are eager to make acquaintance with
unusual delights, should be clearly told that they will find
in hashish nothing miraculous, absolutely nothing but an

exaggeration of the natural. The brain and organism on which hashish operates will produce only the normal phenomena peculiar to that individual—increased, admittedly, in number and force, but always faithful to their origin. A man will never escape from his destined physical and moral temperament: hashish will be a mirror of his impressions and private thoughts—a magnifying mirror, it is true, but only a mirror.

Have a look at the drug itself: a green sweetmeat, the size of a nut and singularly odorous—so much so that it provokes a certain disgust and velleities of nausea; as, indeed any odour would do, however pure or even agreeable in itself, if enhanced to its maximum of strength and, so to speak, density. (I may be allowed to remark, in passing, that this last statement has a corollary, that even the most disgusting and revolting scent might perhaps become a pleasure if it were reduced to its minimum of quantity and effluvium.)

Here, then, is happiness! It is large enough to fill a small spoon. Happiness, with all its intoxications, follies and puerilities. You can swallow it without fear—one does not die of it. Your physical organs will be in no way affected. Later on, perhaps, a too frequent consultation of the oracle will diminish your strength of will; perhaps you will be less of a man than you are today. But the retribution is so distant, and the disaster in store for you so difficult to define! What are you risking? A touch of nervous exhaustion tomorrow? Do you not daily risk worse retribution for lesser rewards?

Well, now, your mind is made up. You have even—in order to make the dose stronger and more diffusely effective— melted your rich extract in a cup of black coffee; you have seen to it that your stomach is empty, by postponing your main meal until nine or ten o'clock that evening, in order to give the poison full freedom of action; perhaps in an hour's time you will take, at the most, some thin soup. You now have enough ballast for a long and singular voyage. The steam-whistle has blown, the sails are set, and you have a curious advantage over ordinary travellers—that of not knowing whither you are going. You have made your choice: hurrah for destiny!

I assume that you have chosen your moment for this adventurous expedition. Every perfect debauch calls for perfect leisure. I have told you, moreover, that hashish produces an exaggeration not only of the individual, but also of his circumstances and surroundings. You must, therefore, have no social obligations demanding punctuality or exactitude; no domestic worries; no distressing affair of the heart. This is most important: for any grief or spiritual unrest, any memory of an obligation claiming your attention at a fixed time, would toll like a bell amidst your intoxication and poison your pleasure. The unrest would become an agony, the worry a torture.

If all these indispensable conditions have been observed, so that the moment is propitious; if your surroundings are favourable—a picturesque landscape, for example, or a poetically decorated apartment; and if, in addition, you can look forward to hearing a little music; why, then, all is for the best.

Intoxication with hashish generally falls into three successive phases, quite easy to distinguish. For beginners even the first symptoms of the first phase will be interesting enough. You have heard vague reports of the drug's marvellous effects. Your imagination has preconceived some private notion of them, something in the nature of an ideal form of drunkenness. You are impatient to learn if the reality will match your expectations. This is sufficient to throw you, from the beginning, into a state of anxiety, which to no small extent encourages the infiltration of the victorious and invading poison.

Most novices, of only the first degree of initiation, complain that hashish is slow in taking effect. They wait with childish impatience for it to do so; and then, when the drug does not function quickly enough to suit them, they indulge in a swaggering incredulity, which gives great delight to old initiates, who know just how hashish sets about its work.

The earliest encroachments of the drug, like symptoms of a storm that hovers before it strikes, appear and multiply in the very bosom of this incredulity. The first of them is a sort of irrelevant and irresistible hilarity. Attacks of causeless mirth, of which you are almost ashamed, repeat themselves at frequent intervals, cutting across periods of stupor during which you try in vain to pull yourself together. The simplest words, the most trivial ideas, assume a new and strange guise; you are actually astonished at having hitherto found them so simple. Incongruous and unforeseeable resemblances and comparisons, interminable bouts of punning on words, rough sketches for farces, continually spout from your brain. The demon has you in thrall. It is useless to struggle against this hilarity, which is as painful as a tickle. From time to time you laugh at yourself, at your own silliness and folly; and your companions, if you have such, laugh alike at your condition and at their own. But, since they laugh at you without malice, you laugh back at them without rancour.

This mirth, with its alternating spells of languor and convulsion, this distress in the midst of delight, generally lasts only for a fairly short time. Soon the coherence or your ideas becomes so vague, the conducting filament between your fancies becomes so thin, that only your accomplices can understand you.

And once again, on this question, too, there is no means of ascertaining the truth: perhaps they only think they understand you, and the deception is mutual. This crazy whimsicality, these explosive bursts of laughter, seem like real madness, or at least like a maniac's folly, to anyone who is not in the same state as yourself. Conversely, the self-control, good sense and orderly thoughts of a prudent observer who has abstained from intoxication—these delight and amuse you like a special sort of dementia. Your rôles are inverted: his calmness drives you to extremes of ironic disdain.

How mysteriously comical are the feelings of a man who revels in incomprehensible mirth at the expense of anyone not in the same situation as himself! The madman begins to feel sorry for the sane man; and, from this moment on, the notion of his own superiority begins to gleam on the horizon of his intellect. Soon it will grow, swell and burst upon him like a meteor.

I once witnessed a scene of this sort, which was carried to great lengths. Its grotesque absurdity was intelligible only to such of those present as understood, at least from observing others, the effects of the drug and the enormous difference in pitch that it creates between two supposedly equal intellects.

A famous musician, who knew nothing of the properties of hashish, and perhaps had never even heard of the drug, found himself among a company of whom several persons had been taking it. They tried to make him understand its marvellous effects. He smiled graciously at their fabulous accounts, out of sheer politeness, in the manner of a man willing to make himself agreeable for a few minutes. His disdain was quickly felt by the others, whose perceptions had been sharpened by the poison, and their laughter wounded him. Finally their hilarious outbursts, the puns and strangely altered faces, the whole unhealthy atmosphere irritated him to the point of saying—perhaps more hastily than he might have wished: "This is an evil burden for an artist to take upon himself; moreover, it must be very very fatiguing."

To the others, the comicality of this remark seemed

dazzling. Their joyful merriment was redoubled.

"This *burden* may suit you," said the musician, "but it would not suit me."

"All that matters is whether it suits us," one of the sick company said egotistically.

Not knowing whether he had to do with real madmen, or with people who were shamming madness, the musician thought it best to leave. But somebody locked the door and hid the key. Another person, going on his knees before the musician, begged his pardon, in the name of the company, and informed him, lachrymosely but insolently, that despite his (the musician's) spiritual inferiority, which perhaps excited a little pity, all present were filled with the deepest affection towards him.

The musician resigned himself to remaining, and, at the company's urgent request, was even so good as to play some music. But the sound of the violin, spreading through the room like a new contagion, laid hands (the expression is not too strong) first on one of the sick men and then on another. There were deep, hoarse sighs, sudden sobs, floods of silent tears. The musician grew alarmed, and stopped playing. Going up to the man whose blissful state was causing the greatest hubbub, he asked him whether he was in great pain, and what he (the musician) could do to help him. One of those present, a "practical man", suggested lemonade and stomach-powders. But the sufferer, his eyes shining with ecstasy, looked at them both with unutterable scorn. To think of wishing to "cure" a man sick with superabundance of life, a man sick with joy!

As this anecdote shows, one of the most noticeable sensations resulting from the use of hashish is that of benevolence; a flaccid, idle, dumb benevolence, resulting from a softening of the nerves.

In confirmation of this, somebody once told me of an adventure that had befallen him whilst at this stage of intoxication. Since he had retained a very exact memory of his sensations, I could perfectly understand the grotesque embarrassment in which he had been inextricably involved as a result of that difference in pitch and level of which I was speaking.

I cannot remember whether my informant was having his first or second experience of the drug. Did he take rather too strong a dose, or did the hashish produce, without any apparent cause—this often happens—much more vigorous effects than usual? He told me that, in the midst of his delight (that supreme delight of feeling oneself filled with life, and believing oneself filled with genius), he was all at once seized with terror. After having at first been dazzled by the beauty of his sensations, he was suddenly appalled by them. He asked himself what would become of his intellect and physical faculties if this condition, which seemed to him supernatural, were to grow more and more aggravated; if his nerves were to become continually more and more delicate?

Because of the power of enlargement possessed by the inward eye of the victim, such a fear as this can be an unspeakable torture. "I was like a runaway horse," said my informant, "galloping towards a precipice, trying to halt but unable to do so. It was truly a fearsome gallop; and my thoughts, enslaved by circumstances, situation, accident — by everything implied in the word 'hazard'—had taken a purely rhapsodic turn. 'It is too late!' I kept desperately repeating.

"When this mode of sensation ceased—after what appeared to me an infinity of time, lasting, in fact, perhaps only a few minutes—and I was expecting to be able at last to sink into that state of beatitude, so dear to Orientals, which follows on the phase of furore, I was overwhelmed by a new 'unhappiness'. I was stricken with a new disquiet—this time quite trivial and childish. I suddenly remembered that I had been invited to a formal dinner with a party of respectable people. I foresaw myself in the midst of a discreet, well-behaved crowd, where everybody else would be in full control of his faculties, whilst I myself would be obliged carefully to conceal my mental condition—and under brilliant lamplight! I was fairly confident of being able to do this, but almost swooned at the thought of the efforts of will I should have to exert.

"By I know not what accident, the words of the Gospel 'Woe to him who giveth scandal!' arose in my memory. I tried hard to forget them, but kept ceaselessly repeating them in my mind. My unhappiness (for it was a real unhappiness) assumed grandiose proportions. I resolved, despite my weakness, to pull myself together and consult an apothecary; for I knew nothing of reagents, and proposed to present myself, free and without a care, in the society to which duty called me.

"But at the door of the shop a sudden thought struck me, causing me to stop and consider for a few moments. I had just seen my reflection in a shop window, and the sight of my own face had amazed me. My pallor, my receding lips, my bulging eyes! 'I shall upset the worthy apothecary,' I told myself, 'and for what a silly reason!'

"Another feeling I had was a fear of meeting people in the shop and appearing ridiculous. But all other feelings were dominated by a sense of benevolence towards the unknown apothecary. I thought of him as a man having the same exaggerated sensibilities as I myself had at that terrible moment. I supposed, therefore, that his ear-drums and soul must quiver, as mine did, at the least noise, and I decided to enter his shop on tiptoe. 'I cannot be too careful,' I said to myself, 'in dealing with a man who, in his goodness of heart, will be alarmed at my plight.'

"I also assured myself that I would muffle not only the sound of my steps, but also the sound of my voice. You are acquainted with the voice of hashish? It is grave, deep, guttural, much like the voice of long-addicted opium-eaters.

"The result was the contrary of what I had hoped. In my resolve to reassure the apothecary, I succeeded in scaring him. He knew nothing of my 'illness'; he had never even heard of it. Nevertheless, he looked at me with a curiosity strongly mixed with distrust. Was he taking me for a madman, or for a beggar? Neither the one nor the other, no doubt; but these were the crazy notions that passed through my brain. I felt obliged to explain to him, at great length (and with what weariness!), all about conserve of hemp and the use to which it was put. I continually repeated to him that there was no reason for *him* to be alarmed, and that all I wanted was some palliative or antitoxin. I kept insisting on the sincere regret I felt at my vexatious intrusion.

"Finally—and imagine all the humiliation to which the words subjected me!—the man simply asked me 'please to leave the shop.' This was the reward of my exaggerated charity and benevolence!

"I went to my dinner-party, and created no scandal. Nobody guessed at the superhuman efforts I had to make to be like everyone else. But I shall never forget the tortures of an ultra-poetical intoxication hampered by the need for decorum and thwarted by a sense of duty!"

Although naturally inclined to sympathise with all sufferings that arise from imagination, I could not help laughing at this narrative. The man from whom I had it is not cured. He has continued to demand from the accursed sweetmeat the stimulus that one should find in oneself; but because he is a careful and orderly person, "a man of the world", he has reduced the doses, thus enabling himself to increase their frequency. He will make acquaintance later with the rotten fruits of his dietetic system.

Let me now revert to the normal development of the intoxication. After the first phase of childish mirth comes a sort of momentary lull. But soon new adventures are heralded by a sensation of chilliness in the extremities (for some people this becomes an intense cold), and a great weakness in all the members. In your head, and throughout your being, you feel an embarrassing stupor and stupefaction. Your eyes bulge, as if under the pull, both physical and spiritual, of an implacable ecstasy. Your face is flooded with pallor. Your lips shrink and are sucked back into your mouth by that panting movement that characterises the ambition of a man who is a prey to great projects, overwhelmed by vast thoughts, or gaining breath for some violent effort. The sides of the gullet cleave together, so to speak. The palate is parched with a thirst that it would be infinitely pleasant to satisfy, if only the delights of idleness were not still more agreeable, and did they not forbid the slightest disarrangement of the body's posture. Hoarse, deep sighs burst forth from your chest, as if your *old* body could not endure the desires and activity of your *new* soul. Now and then a jolt passes through you, making you twitch involuntarily. It is like one of those sharp sensations of falling that you experience at the end of a day's work, or on a stormy night just before finally falling asleep.

Before going any further, I would like to recount, concerning the sensation of chilliness that I mentioned above, yet another anecdote, which will serve to show how greatly the drug's effects, even the purely physical ones, can vary between individuals. This time the speaker is a man of letters, and some passages of his narrative betray, I think, signs of a literary temperament.

"I had taken a moderate dose of rich extract," he told me, "and all was going well. The attack of morbid merriment had not lasted long, and I was in a state of languor and stupefaction which was almost one of happiness. I was therefore looking forward to a peaceful and carefree evening.

"Unfortunately I was by chance constrained to accompany someone to a theatre. I bravely faced the task, determined to disguise my immense desire for idleness and immobility. Since all the carriages in my district were engaged, I had to resign myself to a long walk amidst the harsh noises of carriages, the stupid conversations of passers-by, a whole ocean of trivial stupidities.

"I had already begun to feel a slight chilliness in the tips of my fingers. This soon turned into an intense cold, as if both my hands were dipped in a pail of icy water. But this was not a hardship; the almost piercing sensation affected me more as a pleasure. Nevertheless, the cold invaded me more and more with every step I took on this interminable journey.

"Two or three times I asked the person accompanying me if the weather was really very cold. He replied that, on the contrary, the temperature was more than warmish.

"When I was at last installed in the body of the theatre, shut up in the assigned box, with three or four hours of rest in store for me, I felt as if I had arrived in the Promised Land. The feelings that I had been suppressing on the way, with all the poor strength of which I was capable, now burst in upon me, and I abandoned myself to my silent frenzy. The cold became deeper and deeper; yet I saw that other people were lightly clad, or were even wiping their brows.

"I was seized by a delightful notion that I was a man uniquely privileged, alone allowed the right to feel cold in a theatre in summer. The cold increased until it became alarming; but I was principally dominated by a curiosity to know how far the thermometer would fall. Finally it fell to such a point, the cold was so complete and general, that all my ideas froze, so to speak. I was a block of thinking ice. I felt like a statue hewn from an icy slab. This mad illusion provoked in me a pride, a sense of moral well-being, that I cannot describe to you.

"My abominable delight was enhanced by the certain knowledge that none of the spectators was aware of my nature, of my superiority to them. It was gleeful to think that my companion did not for an instant suspect what bizarre sensations had possessed me. I held the reward for my dissimulation: my unique form of pleasure was a real secret.

"I should add that, soon after I entered my box, my eyes were assailed by an impression of darkness—which I think is somehow akin to the notion of cold. It is very possible that the two notions mutually strengthen each other.

"As you know, hashish always evokes magnificent illuminations, glorious splendours, cascades of liquid gold. Under its influence, all light is good: light that gushes in floods or clings like tinsel to points and rough surfaces; the light of drawing-room candelabra or the tapers of May; the rose-red avalanches of the setting sun. Here in the theatre, the light emitted by the wretched chandelier seemed quite inadequate to my insatiable thirst for brightness. I appeared to myself to be entering, as I have said, a world of darkness—a darkness that gradually thickened, whilst I dreamt of polar night and everlasting winter.

"The stage itself (the theatre habitually shows farces) was the only patch of light, extremely small and far, far away, as if it were at the end of a huge stereoscope. I shall not try to tell you that I listened to the actors, because you know that this would have been impossible. Occasionally my mind caught hold, in passing, of a shred of phrase, and like a skilled dancer used it as a springboard from which to leap into remote fantasies.

"One might suppose that a play heard in this fashion would lack logic and sequence. Do not make this mistake: I discovered a very subtle meaning in a play created by my errant fancy. Nothing in it took me by surprise: I was like the poet who, on seeing for the first time a performance of 'Esther,' found it quite natural that Haman should make love to the Queen. (This was the poet's interpretation, as you will have realised, of the scene in which Haman flings himself at Esther's feet to beg forgiveness for his crimes.) If all plays were listened to in this fashion they would gain much new beauty—even the plays of Racine.

"The actors seemed to me exceedingly small, and to be clearly and carefully outlined, like figures by Meissonier. I could distinctly see not only the most minute details of their costumes—the patterns of the materials, the needlework, buttons, etc.—but also the dividing line between the make-up and the face, the patches of white, blue and red on their features. These Lilliputians were invested with a cold, magical brightness, like that of a very clean sheet of glass over a painting in oils.

"When I was at last able to emerge from this cave of icy darkness, when my inward fantasmagoria had melted away and I had returned to my proper senses, I felt more exhausted than I have ever been by any spell of intent and pressing work."

As the narrator indicates, it is at this phase of intoxication that a new subtlety or acuity manifests itself in all the senses. This development is common to the senses of smell, sight, hearing and touch. The eyes behold the Infinite. The ear registers almost imperceptible sounds, even in the midst of the greatest din.

This is when hallucinations set in. External objects acquire, gradually and one after another, strange new appearances; they become distorted or transformed. Next occur mistakes in the identities of objects, and transposals of ideas. Sounds clothe themselves in colours, and colours contain music.

"There's nothing at all unnatural about that," the reader will say. "Such correspondences between sounds and colours are easily perceived by a poetic brain in its normal healthy state." But I have already warned the reader that there was nothing positively supernatural about the intoxication of hashish. The difference is that the correspondences take on an unusual liveliness; they penetrate and invade the mind, despotically overwhelming it. Notes of music turn into numbers; and, if you are endowed with some aptitude for mathematics, the melody or harmony you hear, whilst retaining its pleasurable and sensuous character, transforms itself into a huge arithmetical process, in which numbers beget numbers, whilst you follow the successive stages of reproduction with inexplicable ease and an agility equal to that of the performer.

It sometimes happens that your personality disappears, and you develop objectivity—that preserve of the pantheistic poets—to such an abnormal degree that the contemplation of outward objects makes you forget your own existence, and you soon melt into them. Your eye rests upon an harmoniously-shaped tree bowing beneath the wind. Within a few seconds something that to a poet would merely be a very natural comparison becomes to you a reality. You begin by endowing the tree with your own passions, your desire or melancholy; its groanings and swayings become your own, and soon you *are* the tree. In the same way, a bird soaring beneath a blue sky, at first merely *represents* the immortal yearning to soar above human life; but already you are the bird itself.

Let us suppose that you are sitting and smoking. Your gaze rests a moment too long on the bluish clouds emerging from your pipe. The notion of a slow, steady, eternal evaporation will take hold of your mind, and soon you will apply this notion to your own thoughts and your own thinking substance. By a singular transposition of ideas, or mental play upon words, you will feel that you yourself are evaporating, and that your pipe (in which you are huddled and pressed down like the tobacco) has the strange *power to smoke you*.

D

Luckily this apparently interminable fancy has lasted only for a single minute—for a lucid interval, gained with a great effort, has enabled you to glance at the clock. But a new stream of ideas carries you away: it will hurtle you along in its living vortex for a further minute; and this minute, too, will be an eternity, for the normal relation between time and the individual has been completely upset by the multitude and intensity of sensations and ideas. You seem to live several men's lives in the space of an hour. You resemble, do you not? a fantastic novel that is being lived instead of being written. There is no longer any fixed connection between your organs and their powers; and this fact, above all, is what makes this dangerous exercise, in which you lose your freedom, so very blameworthy.

When I speak of hallucinations, the reader must not understand the word in the strictest sense. There is a very important shade of distinction between pure hallucination, as frequently studied by doctors, and the hallucination, or rather derangement, of the senses arising from the mental state due to hashish. In cases of the former, the hallucination is sudden, complete and imposed upon the will; moreover, it has no foundation or excuse in the world of external objects. The sufferer sees shapes, or hears sounds, where there are none. In cases of the latter, the hallucination is progressive and almost willed, and it never becomes complete; it is nourished only by the activity of the imagination. Furthermore, it has a foundation: a sound may speak, utter precise words—but there has been a sound. The intoxicated gaze of a man under the influence of hashish will see strange shapes—but, before they became strange and monstrous, these shapes were simple and natural.

The force, the literally *speaking* intensity, of hallucination due to hashish in no way contradicts the fact of the basic difference between the two kinds. Hallucination due to hashish has roots in physical surroundings and the present time; pure hallucination has none.

To convey a better understanding of this seething of the imagination, this ripening of the dream, this poetic accouchement to which a brain intoxicated by hashish is condemned, I shall recount a further anecdote. This time the narrator is not a young man of leisure, nor yet a man of letters, but a woman—a woman of slightly mature age, a seeker after new things, a person readily excitable. Having yielded to her desire to make acquaintance with the poison, she wrote to another lady, describing the principal of her visions (I copy from her letter, word for word):

"However strange and new may have been the sensations that I derived from my twelve-hour folly (was it twelve or twenty? I truly don't know!), I shall never indulge in it again. The mental excitement is too lively, and the resulting fatigue too great; and, to put it shortly, I consider that this deliberate return to childhood has something criminal about it.

"At last I gave in to my curiosity. After all, it was a folly shared with others, in the house of some old friends, amongst whom I saw no great harm in a slight loss of my dignity.

"I must first of all tell you that this accursed hashish is very treacherous stuff. You sometimes think that you have shaken off the intoxication, but it is only a deceptive lull. There are periods of rest, then renewed attacks.

"Towards ten o'clock in the evening I found myself enjoying one of these momentary respites, and thought myself delivered from that superabundance of vitality which had, it is true, given me much delight, but had also brought with it no little uneasiness and fear. I sat down to supper with pleasure, like one weary after a long voyage; for until then, as a precaution, I had abstained from eating.

"But before I had even risen from table, the delirium seized me again, as a cat seizes a mouse; and again the poison began toying with my poor brain. Although my house is quite near my friends' residence, and there was a carriage waiting for me, I felt so much overwhelmed by the need to dream and abandon myself to the irresistible mania that I joyfully accepted their offer to keep me with them until the next day.

"You know my friends' house; you know that they have decorated, furnished and 'done up' in modern style all the part lived-in by the family, but that the part usually uninhabited has been left as it was, with the old furniture and decorations. They decided to improvise a bed-room for me in this latter part of the house, and selected for the purpose the smallest room, a sort of boudoir, rather faded and decrepit, but none the less charming. I must describe it to you as best I can, to enable you to understand the singular vision to which I was victim for the space of a whole night—although I had no leisure to notice the passage of the hours.

"The boudoir is very small and confined. At the level of the cornice, the ceiling curves into an arch. The walls are covered with long, narrow mirrors separated by panels covered with landscapes painted in the slapdash style of stage-settings. Along the cornice, on all four walls, are various allegorical figures, some in restful attitudes and others running or hovering. Above these are brilliant birds and flowers. Behind the figures rises a painted imitation of a lattice, following the curve of the ceiling.

"The ceiling itself is gilt. This means that all the interstices between the baguettes and the figures are covered with gold, and at the centre of the ceiling the gilding is interrupted only by the geometrical network of the sham lattice.

"As you see, the whole affair was rather like a very elegant cage—a very fine cage for a very big bird.

"I should add that the night was also very fine—very clear, with a very bright moon; so that, even after I had snuffed the candle, all this setting was still visible: not illuminated by my imagination, as you might suppose, but lit up by the fine night, whose radiance clung to all the tracery of gilding, mirrors and motley colours.

"I was at first much astonished to see vast spaces stretching out before me, to right and left, in all directions—transparent rivers and green landscapes reflected in quiet waters. You can guess the effect of the panels ceaselessly repeated in the mirrors.

"When I looked above my head, I saw a sunset like molten metal cooling off. This was the gilding of the ceiling; but the lattice-work made me think I was in a kind of cage, or in a house opening on all sides onto space, and that I was separated from all the wonders outside only by the bars of my magnificent gaol.

"At first I laughed at this illusion; but the more I looked, the more the witchery grew, the more the scene assumed life, clarity and an overmastering reality.

"Soon the idea of encagement took dominion over my spirit—without interfering too much, I should mention, with the varied pleasures that I obtained from the spectacle displayed above and around me. I thought that I was to be shut up for a long time, thousands of years, perhaps, in this sumptuous cage, amidst these faery landscapes, between these wondrous horizons. I thought dreamily about the Sleeping Beauty, about an ordained expiation and a future deliverance.

"Above my head flitted brilliant tropical birds. Then, as my ear caught the sound of bells on the necks of horses on the highroad, my senses of sight and hearing coalesced their perceptions into a single image: I thought that the birds were singing, with metal throats, a mysterious, coppery song. It was obvious that they were talking about me, rejoicing in my captivity. Gambolling monkeys and clowning satyrs seemed to be laughing at the prostrate prisoner, condemned to immobility.

"Meanwhile, however, all the mythological divinities were gazing at me with charming smiles, as if to encourage me to endure the spell patiently; the irises of their eyes slid over into the corners of their eyelids, as if to catch my glance. I concluded that if, on the one hand, certain ancestral faults, sins of which I knew nothing, had necessitated this temporary punishment, I could, on the other hand, rely upon the sublime goodness which, whilst sentencing me to suffer for an as yet indeterminate period, would offer me pleasures more serious than the doll's delights that occupy our youth.

"As you see, moral reflections also played a part in my dream. But I must confess that the pleasure of contemplating these brilliant shapes and colours, and believing myself to be the centre of a fantastic drama, frequently absorbed all my other thoughts.

"This condition lasted a long time, a very long time. . . . . Did it last until the morning? I do not know. Suddenly I saw the morning sun shining through my room. I felt a lively astonishment, and, despite all my efforts to remember, I could not tell whether I had slept or had patiently endured a delightful insomnia. A moment ago, it had been night—and now it was day! Yet in the meanwhile I had lived a long, oh! a very long time. . . . . Having lost the notion of time, or rather, the power of measuring time, I had been able to measure the passing of the entire night only by the multitude of my thoughts. Long though it seemed to have been, by this calculation, yet it also seemed to have lasted only a few seconds, or even to have had no place in eternity at all.

"I shall not describe to you the fatigue . . . . . it was immense. The inspiration of poets and creators is said to resemble what I experienced—although I have always imagined that people whose business it is to stir our emotions ought themselves to have very calm temperaments. But if the delirium of the poet really resembles what I obtained

from a small spoonful of conserve, I think that the poet has
to pay very dearly for the public's pleasure. It was not
without a certain sense of well-being, a prosaic satisfaction,
that I felt myself to be 'home' again, in my intellectual
'home'—that is to say, in real life."

This is clearly a woman of good sense. But we shall use her
story only to extract from it a few useful observations,
which will complete this very summary description of the
chief sensations engendered by hashish.

She spoke of supper as having been a pleasure arriving at
a very good moment, just when a lull, temporary but
seemingly permanent, was enabling her to return to real
life. As I have said, such respites and deceptive calms do
occur; and hashish often awakens a voracious hunger, and
almost always an excessive thirst. The trouble is that dinner
or supper, instead of bringing permanent relief, creates a
new paroxysm, an attack of dizziness such as the lady
complained of, followed by a series of bewitching visions,
lightly tinged with fear—to which she resigned herself
deliberately and with very good grace.

The hunger and thirst take some labour to appease, since
a man feels himself so much elevated above material things—
or, to be more exact, is so incapacitated by his intoxication—
that he has to spend a long time in plucking up the courage
to lift a bottle or fork.

The convulsion provoked by the taking of food is indeed
very violent. It is impossible to struggle against it; and such
a condition would be unendurable if it went on too long,
and did not soon give place to a further phase of the intoxication, which, in the case cited, expressed itself in visions that
were splendid, mildly terrifying and at the same time
offering great consolations. This condition is what Orientals
call the "kief". There is no longer any vertigo or tumult,
but a calm and motionless beatitude, a glorious resignation.
For a long time you have not been your own master, but

this no longer disturbs you. Grief and the notion of time have disappeared—or, if they sometimes raise their heads, they are invariably transfigured by the dominant sensation, and are, in relation to their normal form, what poetic melancholy is to actual grief.

But the chief thing to notice in the lady's story—and this is why I copied it out—is that the hallucination is of bastard origin, since it derives its being from the world of appearances. The mind is only a mirror in which the surroundings are extravagantly reflected.

The next thing to observe is the intervention of what I would like to call the "moral" hallucination: the subject believes himself or herself to be making an expiation. But the feminine temperament, which is little given to analysis, did not allow this lady to observe the singularly optimistic character of her hallucination. The benevolent gaze of the Olympian divinities is poeticised by an essentially "hashish-ine" gloss. I shall not say that the lady actually succeeded in skirting round the edge of remorse; but her thoughts, after turning for a moment to melancholy and regret, were quickly coloured by hope. This is an observation that we shall have further occasion to verify.

She spoke of the fatigue on the following day. This fatigue is, indeed, very great; but it does not make itself felt immediately; and when at last you are compelled to acknowledge its presence, you do so with some surprise. For the first feeling you have, once you have perceived that a new day has dawned on the horizon, is one of astonishing well-being; you seem to enjoy a marvellous mental agility. But, as soon as you are on your feet, a last remnant of the intoxication follows you and impedes your movements, like a ball and chain left over from your recent slavery. Your feeble legs carry you only timidly along, and at every moment you are afraid of breaking yourself, as if you were a brittle object. A great languor (there are people who claim that this, too, has its charms¹ seizes on your mind and spreads through your faculties, like a fog over a landscape.

So there you are, for several hours more, incapable of work, action or energy. This is the punishment for the impious prodigality with which you have squandered your nervous fluid. You have scattered your personality to the twelve winds—and now what trouble you will have in putting it together again!

IV

MAN BECOME GOD

It is time to say farewell to all these conjuror's tricks, to these great puppets born of the fumes of infantile brains. Have we not something graver to discuss: the effects of hashish upon human sentiments—its *moral* effects, in short?

Hitherto I have merely been compiling an abridged monograph on the intoxication itself; I have confined myself to emphasising its main features, especially the material ones. But what will seem more important, I think, to a man of spiritual discernment is to understand the poison's action upon man's spiritual part—the enlargement, distortion and exaggeration of his normal sentiments and moral perceptions until they present, in this unusual atmosphere, a real phenomenon of refraction.

A man who, after having long been in the power of opium or hashish, has succeeded, despite his enfeeblement by the habit of slavery, in mustering the necessary energy for his deliverance, seems to me like an escaped prisoner. He inspires me with more admiration than the prudent man who has never lapsed, having always been careful to avoid temptation.

The English frequently use, when speaking of opium-eaters, terms that will seem excessive only to innocents who know nothing of the horrors of this downfall: "enchained," "fettered," "enslaved." * Chains, indeed, in comparison with which all other chains—those of duty or lawless passion—are ribbons of gauze, spider's webs! An appalling thing, the marriage of a man to himself!

"I had become a slave to opium. It had me in its clutches, and all my work and my plans had taken on the colour of my dreams," † says the husband of Ligeia. But in how many marvellous passages does Edgar Poe, that incomparable poet and unrefuted philosopher, who should always be quoted on all the mysterious maladies of the soul, describe the sombre and compelling splendours of opium! The lover of radiant Berenice, Aegeus, the metaphysician, speaks of an alteration in his faculties that constrains him to attach an abnormal and monstrous importance to the most simple phenomena. "To ponder indefatigably for long hours, with my attention rivetted upon some childish observation on the margin or in the text of a book—to stay absorbed, for the greater part of a summer day, in observing a strange shadow obliquely lengthening itself across the carpet or wooden floor—to spend a whole night of forgetfulness watching the erect flame of a lamp, or the glowing embers of a hearth—to dream for whole days about the scent of a flower—monotonously to repeat some trivial word until its sound, by dint of repetition, ceased to have any meaning for the mind—these were some of the commonest and least pernicious aberrations of my mental faculties; aberrations that are doubtless not unprecedented, but certainly defy any explanation or analysis."

There is also the neurotic Augustus Bedloe, who takes his dose of opium every morning, before going for a walk, and

---

* These three words are in English in the original.
† This and the subsequent passages from E. A. Poe have been translated back into English from the French.

assures us that the chief benefit he derives from this daily self-poisoning is that of taking an exaggerated interest in everything, even in the most trivial things: "Meanwhile the opium had had its customary effect, which is to invest the whole outer world with an intensity of interest. In the trembling of a leaf—the colour of a blade of grass—the shape of a clover—the buzzing of a bee—the brilliance of a dewdrop —the sigh of the wind—the vague scents from a wood—was produced a whole world of inspirations, a magnificent and motley procession of disordered and rhapsodic thoughts."

So speaks, through the mouth of his characters, the master of horror, the prince of mystery. These two descriptions of the effects of opium are also completely applicable to those of hashish. In both cases, the intelligence, formerly free, becomes a slave; but the word "rhapsodic", which so well portrays a train of thoughts suggested and dictated by the outer world and the hazard of circumstance, has a great and more terrible truth in relation to hashish. Here the reason becomes mere flotsam, at the mercy of all currents, and the train of thought is *infinitely more* accelerated and "rhapsodic".

This is, I think, a sufficiently clear proof that hashish is much more vehement than opium in its immediate effects, much more of an enemy to orderly existence—in short, much more subversive. I do not know whether ten years of addiction to hashish will bring on disasters equal to those caused by ten years of opium-eating. I say only that, in the immediate present and its morrow, the results of hashish are more deadly. Opium is a peaceful seducer; hashish is a disorderly demon.

I propose, in this last section of my essay to describe and analyse the moral ravages caused by this dangerous and delightful course of exercise: ravages so great, and a danger so profound, that those who return from the fight only lightly injured seem to me like brave men who have escaped from the cave of a multiform Proteus; like Orpheuses victorious over Hell.

You may regard such words, if you wish, as an exaggerated metaphor; but I shall assert that the stimulant poisons are, in my opinion, not only one of the most terrible and surest means at the disposal of the Prince of Darkness for the recruitment and subjugation of deplorable humanity, but actually one of his most perfect embodiments.

At this point, in order to lessen my task and clarify my analysis, I shall cease compiling disparate anecdotes, and instead assemble a mass of observations around a single fictitious individual. I must therefore create for this purpose a personality of my own choosing.

In his *Confessions*, De Quincey rightly states that opium, far from sending a man to sleep, actually stimulates him; but that it stimulates him only to follow his own natural bent; so that, in order to expound the wonders of opium, it would be absurd to describe the experiences of a cattle-dealer—for such a man would dream only of cattle and grazing-grounds. I have no need, therefore, to describe the heavy fantasies of an intoxicated stockman; for who would get any pleasure from reading about them, or would consent to do so?

To create a general picture of my subject, I must focus all its rays within a single circle; I must polarise them. And the tragic circle within which I shall assemble them will be, as I have said, a personality of my own choosing: something analogous to what the eighteenth century called "the man of sensibility" and the Romantics "the misunderstood genius"; or what families and the mass of citizenry today generally stigmatise as "an original".

A temperament half nervous and half choleric—such is the one most favourable to the evolutions of the intoxication that we are discussing. Let us add to this a cultivated mind, practised in the study of form and colour; and a tender heart, wearied by unhappiness but still ready for rejuvenescence. We shall even, if you insist, go so far as to admit the presence of certain old weaknesses, and—as their inevitable consequence, in an easily excitable nature—moments of what may or may not be positive remorse, but is at least a regret for profaned and ill-spent time. We may usefully add a taste for metaphysics and an acquaintance with the various basic theories of philosophy concerning human destiny; also that love of virtue—abstract virtue, either stoical or mystical—which is advocated, in all the books that nowadays provide the spiritual nourishment of adolescence, as the highest summit that a noble soul can attain. If we add to all this a great subtlety of the senses—which I have omitted as supererogatory—I think that I have assembled all the general elements common to the man of sensibility in our time: what might be called "the ordinary sort of eccentric".

Let us now see what happens to such a personality when driven to desperate extremes by hashish. Let us follow the procession of the human imagination to its last and most magnificent altar, to the individual's belief in his own godhead.

If you are such a soul, your innate love of form and colour will find, to start with, a huge pasture in the first developments of your intoxication. Colours assume an unusual force and enter your brain with a conquering intensity. Whether fine or mediocre, or even bad, paintings on ceilings take on a terrifying life; the crudest wallpapers in the commonest inn recede into splendid dioramas. Nymphs with brilliant bodies gaze at you with eyes deeper and clearer than sky or water; famous characters of antiquity, attired in their sacerdotal or military garb, manage by their looks alone to exchange solemn confidences with you. The convolutions of outlines are a definite and clear language, in which you read the agitations and desires of human souls.

Meanwhile you develop that mysterious and temporary state of mind in which life in all its depth, bristling with its manifold problems, reveals itself in its entirety upon whatever scene, however ordinary or trivial, presents itself to your eyes; a scene in which the first object you see becomes an eloquent symbol. Fourier and Swedenborg, the former with his "analogies" and the latter wtih his "correspondencies", embody themselves in the flora and fauna upon which your glance falls. Instead of instructing you in words, they indoctrinate you with form and colour.

Your understanding of allegory assumes proportions hitherto unknown to yourself. (We may observe in passing that allegory—a deeply spiritual art-form, which, although incompetent painters have accustomed us to despise it, is really one of the primitive and most natural forms of poetry —regains, in an intellect enlightened by hashish, its legitimate dominion.) Hashish spreads over the whole of life a sort of veneer of magic, colouring it with solemnity and shining through all its depths. Scalloped landscapes; fleeting horizons; perspectives of towns blanched by the cadaverous pallor of a storm or illumined by the concentrated glows of sunset, depths of space, allegorical of the depths of time; the dances, movements or utterances of actors (if you happen to have fetched up in a theatre); the first phrase that catches your eye, if you glance at a book: everything in short, the universality of all existence, arrays itself before you in a new and hitherto unguessed-at glory.

Even grammar, dry-as-dust grammar, becomes something like a sorcerer's conjuration. The words are resurrected in flesh and bone: the noun, in its substantial majesty, the adjective, the transparent robe that clothes and colours the noun like a glorious burnish; the verb, angel of motion, that gives a sentence its impetus.

Music, another form of speech beloved by the lazy, or by deep minds seeking relaxation in a charge of activity, tells you about yourself, recites to you the poem of your life. It enters bodily into you, and you in turn become dissolved in it. It tells of your passions—not in a vague, indefinite manner, as it does at a casual evening's entertainment, or during a visit to the opera, but circumstantially and positively, with each movement of the rhythm recording a well-known movement of your soul, and with the entire poem entering your brain, like a dictionary that has come alive.

It must not be supposed that all these phenomena arise in the mind pell-mell, with the shrieking accent of reality and all the disorderliness of the outer world. The inward eye transforms everything, giving to each phenomenon the beauty that it must have if it is to be truly worthy of our delight.

To this essentially hedonistic and sensuous phase belongs, too, the love of clear waters, running or still, that grows so astonishingly amidst the mental intoxication to which some artists are subject. Mirrors become occasions for a daydream that is like a thirst of the soul, conjoined with that physical, throat-parching thirst of which I have already spoken. Fleeting eddies, the frolics of water, harmonious cascades, the sea's blue immensity, all these surge by you, singing and sleeping, with an inexpressible charm. The water gleams like a very enchantress—so that, although I do not greatly believe in the furious fancies of hashish, I should not assert that the contemplation of a limpid gulf was without danger for a soul in love with crystalline space; or that the ancient fable of Undine might not become for the devotee a tragic reality.

I think I have already said enough concerning the monstrous expansion of time and space—two ideas that are always connected, but which a mind in this condition contemplates without sorrow or fear. Such a mind gazes, with a certain melancholic delight, down through the depths of the years, and boldly plunges into infinite perspectives.

The reader will, I suppose, have already guessed that this abnormal and tyrannical expansion applies itself equally to all sentiments and ideas. To benevolence, for example—I have given a fairly illustrative example of this; or to love.

In a temperament such as I have taken for my subject, the idea of beauty must naturally have a great place. Harmony symmetry of line, eurhythmics of movement, appear to the dreamer as necessities, as *duties;* not only for all created beings, but also for himself, the dreamer, who finds, at this period of the bout, that he is endowed with a marvellous ability to understand the immortal rhythm of the universe.

If our fanatic lacks beauty in his own person, it must not be supposed that the forced recognition of this fact causes him any prolonged suffering, or that he regards himself as a discordant note in the world of harmony and beauty improvised by his imagination. The sophistries of hashish are many and admirable, with a general tendency towards optimism; and one of the principal sophistries—the most efficacious of them all—is that which transforms desire into reality. The same thing often occurs, no doubt, in ordinary life; but with how much more enthusiasm and subtlety does it occur in the present case! Besides, how could a being so well equipped to understand harmony—a sort of priest of Beauty—form an exception to, or blemish upon, his own cult? Beauty of the soul, with all its puissance; grace of the spirit, with all its powers of seduction; eloquence, with all its feats of prowess: all these ideas hasten to his aid—at first as correctives to an inopportune ugliness; then as comforters; and finally as the perfect flatterers before an imaginary throne.

What about love-making? I have often heard people actuated by a schoolboy inquisitiveness ask some such question of experienced hashish-takers. What can become of the intoxication of love, powerful though it be in a man's natural state, when shut within th's other intoxication, like a sun within a sun? This is the question that arises in the mob-minds of those whom I shall call the street-corner loungers of intellectual society. For the answer to the smutty underlying suggestion—to the part of the question that dares not reveal itself—I shall refer the reader to Pliny, who has somewhere written of the properties of hemp in such a way as to dispel many an illusion on the subject.

It is well known, of course, that the most common result of a man's abuse of his nerves, and of nervous stimulants, is impotence. Since, then, we are not here considering physical potency, but emotion or susceptibility, I shall merely ask the reader to remember that the imagination of a sensitive man, intoxicated moreover with hashish, is tremendously enhanced and as unpredictable as the utmost possible wind-force of a hurricane; and that his senses have been refined to a point almost equally difficult to determine. It is therefore permissible to suppose that a light caress of the most innocent description—a handshake, for example—may have its effect multiplied a hundred times by the state of the recipient's soul and senses, and may perhaps conduce, even quite rapidly, to that syncope which is regarded by vulgar mortals as the *summum bonum*.

What is indisputable, however, is that, in an imagination frequently occupied by thoughts of love, hashish awakens tender memories to which sorrow and misfortune actually lend a new lustre.

It is no less certain that a strong element of sensuality is admixed with these spiritual commotions. And it is worth mentioning, as sufficient evidence of the hashish-taker's immorality in this respect, that a sect of the Ishmaelites (who were the spiritual descendants of the Assassins) carried their worship of the ambisexual lingam to such excess as to make a sole and exclusive cult of the feminine half of the symbol.

It would, therefore, be entirely natural—since every man carries the whole of history within himself—to find some obscene heresy, some monstrous cult, reproducing itself in a mind that has flaccidly yielded itself to the mercy of a hellish drug and smiles at the ruin of its own faculties.

We have seen how the intoxication carries with it a remarkable benevolence, even towards strangers—a sort of philanthropy composed more of pity than of love (it is here that we find the first germ of the satanic spirit that will later grow in so extraordinary a fashion), and amounting to a fear of hurting anyone whomsoever. One can guess that this may become a localised sentimentality, applied to some beloved person who plays, or has played, an important part in the patient's moral life. The cult and adoration of the beloved, the prayers and dreams of bliss, break out with the ambitious force and brilliance of a display of fireworks; and, like the gunpowder and colouring substances of the display, they fade and vanish in the darkness.

There is no sort of combination of the sentiments to which the pliable love of a slave to hashish cannot lend itself. A pleasant sense of giving protection, a feeling of ardent and devoted fatherliness, can be mingled with a disgraceful sensuality, for which hashish will always find excuse and absolution.

It goes still further. Let us suppose that the subject has committed faults which have left traces of bitterness in his soul; that he is a husband or lover who, in his normal state, must feel regret whenever he contemplates a somewhat stormy past. Now this bitterness can be changed to sweetness; the need for pardon makes the imagination more adroit, more suppliant; and remorse itself—in this diabolic drama, which takes the form of a long monologue—can be a stimulant, powerfully rekindling the heart's enthusiasm.

Yes, remorse! Was I wrong in saying that to a truly philosophic mind hashish must seem the perfect instrument of Satan? Remorse, that odd ingredient of pleasure, is soon drowned in the delicious contemplation of remorse, in a sort of voluptuous self-analysis; and this analysis is so rapid that man—this devil by nature, to use the Swedenborgian phrase—does not realise how involuntary it is, or how, second by second, he is approaching perfect diabolism. He *admires* his remorse, he glories in himself, even as his freedom slips away.

So by this time my hypothetical man, this soul of my choosing, has reached the pitch of joy and serenity at which he is *compelled* to admire himself. Every contradiction effaces itself, all the problems of philosophy become crystal-clear, or at least appear to be so. Everything is a matter for rejoicing. The fullness of his life at this moment inspires him with a disproportionate pride. A voice speaks within him (alas! it is his own), saying to him: "You are now entitled to consider yourself superior to all men; nobody knows, or could understand, all that you think and feel; men would be incapable even of appreciating the benevolence with which they inspire you. You are a king unrecognised by the passers-by, a king who lives in the solitude of his own certainty. But what do you care? Do you not possess that sovereign pride which so ennobles the soul?"

We may, however, suppose that now and then a mordant memory pierces and spoils this happiness. Some suggestion furnished by the outer world may recall to life a past that it is disagreeable to contemplate. With how many stupid or base actions is this past not filled—actions truly unworthy of this king of thought, actions that sully his ideal dignity? I assure you that the man of hashish will courageously face these reproachful phantoms and will even succeed in finding in his ugly memories new causes of pleasure and pride.

His train of thought will be as follows: once the first pang of regret has passed, he will analyse with keen interest the action or sentiment whose memory has disturbed his self-glorification; the motives that caused him to behave thus; and the circumstances to which he was subject. And, if he cannot find in these circumstances sufficient grounds for the absolution, or even for extenuation, of his sin, do not suppose that he feels defeated! Let us scrutinise his reasoning, as if it were a mechanism working behind a pane of glass: "This ridiculous, cowardly or base action, whose memory has for a moment upset me, is in complete contradiction to my true nature—my present nature; and the very energy with which I condemn it, the inquisitorial care with which I analyse it and pass judgment upon it, are a proof of my high and divine aptitude for virtue. How many men are there in the world so ready as I am to pass judgment on themselves, so severe in self-condemnation?" Thus he at once condemns and glorifies himself.

Having thus absorbed the horrid memory into his contemplation of ideal virtue, ideal charity, ideal genius, he frankly yields himself to his triumphant orgy of the spirit. We have seen how, sacrilegiously counterfeiting the sacrament of penitence, since he himself is both penitent and confessor, he either gives himself an easy absolution or, worse still, finds in his self-condemnation a new pasture for his pride. Now, from the contemplation of his virtuous dreams and projects, he deduces his practical aptitude for virtue. The sentimental energy with which he embraces his phantom of virtue seems to him a sufficient and commanding proof that he has the virile strength necessary for the attainment of his ideal. He completely confounds dream with action; his imagination kindling more and more at the enchanting spectacle of his own nature corrected and idealised, he substitutes this fascinating image of himself for his real individuality—so poor in strength of will and so rich in vanity—and ends by decreeing his own apotheosis in the following clear and simple words, which contain for him a whole world of abominable delights: "*I am the most virtuous of all men.*"

Doesn't all this remind you of Jean-Jacques, who also, after making his confession to the universe—not without a certain voluptuous pleasure—dared to utter the same shout of triumph (or one very little different), with the same sincerity and conviction? The enthusiasm with which he admired virtue, the nervous sentimentality that filled his eyes with tears at the sight of a noble deed, or at the thought of all the noble deeds he would have liked to perform, sufficed to give him a superlative idea of his own moral worth. Jean-Jacques managed to intoxicate himself without hashish.

Shall I continue the analysis of this conquering monomania? Shall I explain how, under the dominion of the poison, our man soon makes himself the centre of the universe? How he becomes a living and outrageous personification of the proverb which says that desire knows no barriers? He believes in his own virtue and genius: can the end not be guessed? All surrounding objects are so many suggestions provoking in him a world of thought, all more highly coloured, more vivid and more subtle than ever before and clad in a veneer of magic. "These magnificent cities," he tells himself, "with their superb buildings echelonned as if on a stage—these handsome ships swaying on the waters of the harbour in nostalgic idleness, seeming to express my very thought: *When shall we set out for happiness?*"—these museums crammed with lively shapes and intoxicating colours—these libraries where all the works of Science and the dreams of the Muses are assembled —these massed instruments speaking with a single voice— these enchanting women, made still more charming by the science of self-adornment and the demureness of their glances—all these things were created *for me, for me, for me!* For me humanity has worked, been martyrised and immolated—to provide pasture, pabulum to my implacable appetite for emotion, knowledge and beauty!"

Let us hasten on and cut the story short. Nobody will be surprised that a final, supreme thought bursts from the dreamer's brain: *"I have become God!"*; that a wild and ardent shout breaks from his bosom with such force, such projectile power that, if the wishes and beliefs of a drunken man had any effective virtue, this shout would bowl over the angels scattered on the paths of Heaven: *"I am a God!"*

Soon, however, this hurricane of pride dies down into a weather of calm, silent, restful beatitude. All creation is richly coloured, as if illumined by a sulphurous dawn. If by chance a vague memory slips into the soul of the deplorable ecstatic: *"Might there not be another God?,"* you may be sure that he will squarely confront *that other*, discuss his intentions and face him without terror.

Who is the French philosopher who said, satirising modern German doctrines, "I am a god who has had a bad dinner?" This piece of irony would not prick a man carried away by hashish; he would tranquilly answer: "I may have had a bad dinner, but I am a God."

V

MORAL

But the morrow! The terrible morrow! All the body's organs lax and weary, nerves unstrung, itching desires to weep, the impossibility of applying oneself steadily to any task—all these cruelly teach you that you have played a forbidden game. Hideous Nature, stripped of yesterday's radiance, resembles the melancholy debris of a banquet.

The especial victim is the will, that most precious of all the faculties. It is said, and is almost true, that hashish has no evil physical effects; or, at worst, no serious ones. But can it be said that a man incapable of action, good only for dreaming, is truly well, even though all his members may be in their normal condition?

We understand enough of human nature to know that a man who, with a spoonful of conserve, can instantaneously procure for himself all the benefits of heaven and earth, will never earn a thousandth part of these by toil. Can one imagine a State of which all the citizens intoxicated themselves with hashish? What citizens, what warriors and legislators! Even in the East, where its use is so widespread, there are governments that have understood the necessity of banning it. The fact is that man is forbidden, on pain of intellectual ruin and death, to upset the primordial conditions of his existence, to break the equilibrium between his faculties and the surroundings in which they are destined to function—to upset his destiny, in short, and substitute for it a fatality of a new order.

Let us remember Melmoth, that admirable symbol. His appalling suffering lies in the disproportion between his marvellous faculties, acquired instantaneously by a pact with Satan, and the surroundings in which, as God's creature, he is condemned to live. And none of those whom he seeks to seduce is willing to purchase from him, on the same conditions, his own terrible privilege.

It is a fact that any man who does not accept the conditions of human life sells his soul. One can readily perceive the relationship between the satanic creations of poets and those living creatures who have enslaved themselves to the stimulant drugs. The man wished to be God—and soon we see him, by an inexorable moral law, fallen lower than his real nature. He is a soul selling itself piece-meal.

Balzac clearly thought that man's greatest disgrace and keenest suffering is the surrender of his will-power. I once saw him at a gathering at which there was a discussion of the miraculous effects of hashish. He listened and asked questions with an amusing attentiveness and vivacity. Anyone who ever knew him will guess that he must have been keenly interested. But the notion of letting his thoughts pass beyond his own control shocked him deeply. He was shown some dawamesk; he examined it, sniffed it, and passed it back without touching it. His inner conflict, between his almost childish eagerness for knowledge and his loathing of self-surrender, was revealed on his expressive countenance in a most striking fashion. His love of human dignity won the day. It would, indeed, be difficult to imagine this believer in the will, this spiritual twin of Louis Lambert, consenting to lose a particle of this precious "substance."

Despite the admirable services rendered by ether and chloroform, it seems to me that, considered from the point of view of transcendental philosophy, all modern inventions that tend to diminish human liberty, and the pain indispensably bound up with it, are open to the same reproach. It was not without a certain admiration that I once heard a paradoxical comment made by an officer who was telling me of a cruel operation performed at El-Aghouat on a French general, who died of it despite the use of chloroform. This general was a very brave man, and even something more than that—one of those souls to whom the epithet "chivalrous" is naturally applied. "It wasn't chloroform that the general needed," said the officer, "but the gaze of the whole army, and regimental music. Perhaps, with these, he would have been saved!" The surgeon did not share this officer's opinion; but certainly the chaplain would have admired his sentiments.

It is truly superfluous, after all that has been said here, to insist on the immorality of hashish. If I compare it to suicide, a slow suicide, a weapon that is always sharp and bloody, no reasonable person will wish to contradict me. If I liken it to sorcery or magic, those arts that seek—by operating upon matter, and by occult methods whose falsity is proved by nothing so much as by their very effectiveness—

to win an empire forbidden to man, or permitted only to him who is judged worthy, no philosophic soul will have fault to find with this comparison. When the Church condemns magic and sorcery, it is because these militate against the intentions of God; because they blot out the work of time and seek to make superfluous the disciplines of purity and morality; and because she, the Church, regards only those riches as legitimate and genuine that are earned by assiduous seeking.

To describe a gambler who has found a method of betting on a certainty, we use the term "swindler". What shall we call a man who seeks to buy happiness and genius for a small sum of money? It is the very infallibility of the method that constitutes its immorality; just as it is the alleged infallibility of magic that imposes upon it the stigma of hell. I need scarcely add that hashish, like all other solitary delights, makes the individual useless to mankind, and also makes society unnecessary to the individual, who is driven ceaselessly to admire himself, and is daily brought nearer to that glittering abyss in which he will gaze upon the face of Narcissus.

But what if, at the price of his dignity, his honour and his powers of free discernment, a man could obtain from hashish great mental benefits—could make of it a machine for thinking, a richly productive instrument? This is a question that I have often heard asked, and I shall now answer it. First of all, as I have explained at length, hashish reveals to the individual nothing except himself. It is true that this individual is, so to speak, enlarged to the power of three; and, since it is also quite true that the memories of his impressions survive the orgy, the hopes of the "utilitarian" theorists might not at first sight seem entirely unreasonable. But I shall beg them to remember that the thoughts of the hashish-taker, from which they count on obtaining so much, are not really so beautiful as they appear under their momentary guise, clad in the tinsel of magic. They have much more of earth than of heaven in them, and owe a great part of their seeming beauty to the nervous excitement and avidity with which the mind hurls itself upon them.

These people's hopes form, therefore, a vicious circle. Let us grant for a moment that hashish gives, or at least augments, genius—they forget that it is in the nature of hashish to weaken the will; so that what hashish gives with one hand it takes away with the other: that is to say, it gives power of imagination and takes away the ability to profit by it. Even if we imagine a man clever and vigorous enough to gain the one without losing the other, we must bear in mind a further and terrible danger, which attaches itself to all habits. They all soon turn into necessities. He who has recourse to poison in order to think will soon be unable to think *without* poison. How terrible the lot of a man whose paralysed imagination cannot function without the aid of hashish or opium!

In all its philosophical investigations the human mind, like the stars in their courses, has to travel in a curve leading back to its point of departure. The conclusion is the closing of a circle.

At the beginning of this essay I spoke of the marvellous state of mind into which a man sometimes finds himself projected, as if by a special dispensation. I said that, in his ceaseless yearning to rekindle his hopes and uplift himself towards the Infinite, man has displayed, in all places and at all times, a frantic predilection for any substances, however dangerous, that might personally exalt him and thus for a moment evoke for him that adventitious paradise upon which all his desires are fixed. And I remarked that this foolhardy instinct, which urges him, all unbeknownst, towards Hell, is of itself a proof of his natural sublimity. But man is not so forsaken, so lacking in honourable means of attaining to Heaven, that he should be obliged to resort to pharmacy or witchcraft. He has no need to sell his soul to pay for the intoxicating caresses and affections of oriental houris. What, after all, is a paradise bought at the price of one's eternal salvation?

I imagine to myself a man—a Brahman, shall I say, a poet or a Christian philosopher—who has scaled the arduous Olympus of the spirit. Around him the Muses of Raphael or Mantegna reward him for his long fastings and constant prayers by joining in their noblest dances and gazing upon him with their gentlest looks and loveliest smiles. The god Apollo, master of all knowledge—he of Francavilla, Albrecht Dürer, Goltzius, whomsoever you please: has not every man who merits it his own Apollo?—is enticing from his bow its most vibrant chords. Below this man, at the foot of the mountain, amidst the briars and the mud, the human herd, the pack of Helots, is grimacing with false delight and howling in the pangs of its poison. And the poet sadly thinks "These unfortunates, who have neither fasted nor prayed, who have refused redemption by toil, are demanding of black magic the means of raising themselves all of a sudden to superhuman existence. The magic makes dupes of them, shedding upon them a false happiness and a false light. Whereas we, the poets and philosophers, have redeemed our souls by unremitting toil and contemplation. By the constant exercise of our wills and the enduring nobility of our devotion we have created for our use a garden of true beauty. Trusting in the Saying that faith moves mountains, we have performed the only miracle for which God has given us leave."

SHORT POEMS IN PROSE

SHORT POEMS IN PROSE

I

THE STRANGER

"Whom do you love best, tell me, you man of enigma?
Your father, your mother, your sister, your brother?"

"I have no father, mother, sister or brother."

"Your friends?"

"You use a word that I have never to this day been able
to understand."

"Your country?"

"I know not on what latitude it lies."

"Beauty?"

"Her I would willingly love, the divine and deathless."

"Gold?"

"I hate it, as you hate God."

"Well, then, what *do* you love, extraordinary stranger?"

"I love the clouds . . . . . passing clouds . . . . over
yonder . . . . . . the wondrous clouds!"

III

THE ARTIST'S CONFITEOR

How penetrating are the autumn dusks! So penetrating
that they hurt! For there are certain delicious sensations
whose vagueness does not dull their intensity. There is no
more steely barb than that of the Infinite.

What delight, to drown one's gaze in the immensity of sky and sea! Solitude, silence, the incomparable purity of the azure! A little sail quivering on the horizon, in its smallness and isolation mimicking my irremediable existence; the monotonous melody of the surf; all these think through me, or I think through them (for amidst the grandeur of daydream, the *I* is quickly lost!); they think, I say, but in music and picture, without arguments, syllogisms or deductions.

Nevertheless, these thoughts, whether they issue from me or spring from objects, soon become too intense. The energy stored within delight creates a positive distress and suffering. My over-taut nerves emit now only grating and painful vibrations.

Now, of a sudden, the depth of the sky appals me, its limpidity exasperates me. The insensibility of the sea, the lack of movement in the whole spectacle, revolts me . . . . . Must I everlastingly suffer, or must I everlastingly flee from beauty? Nature, pitiless enchantress, ever-victorious rival, give me peace! Cease to provoke my desires and my pride! The study of beauty is a duel in which the artist cries out with fear before he is defeated.

V

THE DOUBLE ROOM

A room like a daydream, a truly *spiritual* room, where the still atmosphere is faintly tinted with pink and blue.

Here the soul bathes in an idleness spiced with regret and desire—something crepuscular, bluish and rosy; a dream of delight during an eclipse.

The shapes of the furniture are elongated, prostrate, languishing. The furniture seems to be dreaming. One might suppose it to be endowed with somnambulistic life, like that of vegetation or of minerals. The stuffs speak a dumb language, like that of flowers, skies or sunsets.

The walls are defiled by no abomination of art. Juxtaposed with pure dream, with the unanalysed impression, positive and definitive art is a blasphemy. Here everything has the sufficing clarity and the delicious obscurity of harmony.

An infinitesimal perfume, most exquisitely choice, in which mingles a faint humidity, swims through this atmosphere in which the half-slumbering spirit is lulled amidst the sensations of a conservatory.

Muslin streams down by the windows and bed, gushing in snowy cascades. On the bed lies the Idol, the sovereign of dreams. But how came she here? Who brought her? What magic power has installed her on this throne of daydream and delight?

What does it matter? There she is, and I recognise her.

Yes, I know those eyes whose flame pierces the dusk—those subtle and terrible "ogles", I know them by their terrifying malice! They attract, enthral and devour the gaze of him who unwisely beholds them. I have often studied them, those black stars compelling curiosity and admiration.

To what benevolent demon do I owe these surroundings of mystery, silence, peace and perfumes? Ah, bliss! That which we generally call life has not, even in its happiest extension, anything in common with this supreme life with which I have now made acquaintance, which I savour minute by minute, second by second!

But no, there are no more minutes or seconds. Time has disappeared. It is Eternity that reigns now—an eternity of delights.

But a knock, heavy and terrible, has resounded on the door, and, as one does in dreams of Hell, I feel as if a pickaxe had struck me in the stomach.

Enter a Spectre. It is a bailiff who is here to torture me in the name of law; an infamous concubine who has come to upbraid me with her poverty and add the trivialities of her life to the sorrows of mine; or perhaps a printer's devil demanding the next instalment of a manuscript.

The paradisal room, the Idol, sovereign of dreams—the *Sylphide*, as the great René used to call her—all that magic has disappeared at the Spectre's brutal stroke.

Horror, my memory returns—my memory! Yes, this hovel, this dwelling of everlasting dreariness, is really mine. Mine, this silly furniture, dusty and delapidated; the hearth without flame or live coal, and befouled with spittle; the gloomy windows where the rain has traced furrows in the grime; the manuscripts unfinished or covered with erasures; the calendar, with dates of foreboding underlined in pencil!

And that other-worldly perfume, so intoxicating to my perfected senses, has been replaced, alas, by a fetid odour of tobacco, mixed with some sickening sort of dampness. The whole place has the rancid reek of desolation.

In this world of mine, narrow but crammed with disgust, only one well-known object smiles upon me: the phial of laudanum. An old and terrible mistress—lavish, like all mistresses, alas, with her caresses and betrayals.

Yes, indeed, Time is here again, Time is again the sovereign ruler; and with that hideous dotard has returned all his demoniac train of Memories, Regrets, Spasms, Fears, Agonies, Nightmares, Angers and Neuroses.

And now, you may be sure, the seconds are loudly and solemnly accentuated—each, as it leaps from the clock, saying: "I am Life, insupportable, implacable Life!"

There is only one Second in human Life whose mission it is to announce news of happiness—that "happy release" of which every man is so inexplicably afraid!

Yes, Time rules again; he has resumed his brutal dictatorship. He prods me like an ox, with his two-pronged goad: "Get up, donkey! Sweat, slave! Live, creature of doom!"

VI

TO EVERY MAN HIS OWN CHIMAERA

Under a grey sky, on a wide, dusty plain without roads, without grass, without a thistle or nettle, I met some men walking bent double.

Each of them carried on his back an enormous Chimaera, as heavy as a sack of flour or coal, or as the equipment of a Roman infantryman.

But the monstrous creature was not merely an inert weight. No, it enfolded and crushed its man with its elastic, powerful muscles; it fastened its two great claws into the breast of its mount; and its fabulous head rose above the man's temples like one of those horrific helmets with which ancient warriors hoped to add to the terror of their enemies.

I questioned one of these men, asking him where they were going in this fashion. He answered that he did not know at all, neither he nor the others; but that obviously they must be going somewhere, since they were driven on by an insuperable desire to proceed.

A curious thing to note: none of these travellers seemed to resent the wild beast hanging from his neck and cleaving to his back. Each man seemed to regard it as a part of himself. None of these grave and weary faces betrayed any despair. Under the spiteful bowl of the sky, with their feet wading in the dust of a soil as desolate as this sky, they plodded on with the resigned expressions of men condemned to perpetual hope.

The procession passed me by, and faded away on the horizon at the point where the planet's curving surface escapes from man's inquisitive gaze.

For a few moments I obstinately continued seeking to understand the mystery. But soon Indifference, that irresistible force, closed in upon me; and I found its burden more overwhelming than these men had found their crushing Chimaeras.

X

ONE A.M.

Alone at last! There is no sound but the rattle of a few belated and weary cabs. For a few hours I shall have the privilege of silence, if not of rest. At last the tyranny of the human face has vanished, and I shall suffer only by myself.

So at last I am allowed to relax myself in a bath of darkness. First of all, let me turn the key twice in the lock. I have the notion that this turning of the key will increase my solitude and strengthen the barricades that, for the moment, separate me from the world.

Horrible life! Horrible city! Let me give an account of the day I have spent: seeing several men of letters, one of whom asked me if it is possible to travel to Russia by land (he must have thought that Russia is an island); arguing heatedly with a magazine-editor, who answered all my objections by saying: "We represent the views of respectable people," as if every other periodical were edited by scoundrels; exchanging greetings with some twenty people, of whom fifteen are unknown to me; distributing handshakes, in the same proportion—and that without having taken the precaution of buying a pair of gloves; paying a visit, to kill time during a shower, on a female charlatan who asked me to design a costume for her "as Venus"; paying court to a theatrical producer, who said, as he showed me out: "Perhaps the best thing for you to do would be to get in touch with Z. . . . .; he's the dullest, stupidest and most famous of all my authors; with his help you might be able to achieve something. Go and visit him, and after that we'll see"; boasting (why?) of a number of rascally actions that I've never committed, and denying, like a coward, one or two other misdeeds that I performed gladly—a misfeasance of braggadocio and a crime against human dignity; refusing a friend an easy service, and writing a letter of recommendation for a complete rogue:—ouf! is that really the whole list? Displeased with everybody, displeased with myself, I should like to regain a little self-redemption and self-pride, amidst the silence and solitude of night. Souls of those whom I have loved, souls of those whom I have sung, strengthen and sustain me, keep hence from me the falsehood and corrupting vapours of the world. And do you, O Lord my God, give me grace to produce a few lines of good poetry, so that I may prove to myself that I am not the most abject of men, that I am not inferior to those whom I despise.

XII

CROWDS

Not everybody has the gift of bathing himself in the crowd: finding pleasure in the masses is an art; and the only person who can indulge in a drunken spree of vitality, for which the human race itself foots the bill, is one into whom a fairy has breathed, in his cradle, a love of fancy-dress and masquerades, a hatred of domesticity and a passion for travel.

Multitude, solitude: terms that an active and fertile poet can make equal and interchangeable. A man who does not know how to populate his solitude can as little know how to be alone amidst a busy crowd.

The poet enjoys the incomparable privilege of being, at will, both himself and other people. Like a wandering soul seeking a body, he can enter, whenever he wishes, into anyone's personality. For him alone all seats are vacant; and if some places seem to be closed to him, it is because in his eyes they are not worth the trouble of a visit.

The solitary and meditative rambler obtains an odd sort of intoxication from this general communion of spirits. The man who can readily wed himself with the crowd knows feverish joys that will always be barred to the egoist, shut-up like a strongbox, or the idler, as limited as a mollusc. He takes as his own all the professions, rejoicings and miseries that circumstance brings before him.

What men call love is a very small, restricted and weak thing compared with this ineffable orgy, this holy prostitution of a soul that gives itself utterly, with all its poetry and charity, to the unexpectedly emergent, to the passing unknown.

It is good to teach sometimes the happy ones of this world—if only to humiliate for a moment their foolish pride—that there are pleasures superior to theirs, vaster and more refined. Founders of colonies, pastors of peoples, missionary priests exiled to the end of the earth, doubtless know something of these mysterious intoxications. In the bosoms of the huge families that their genius has created, they must sometimes laugh at the people who express sympathy for them in their precarious and austere lives.

XVI

THE CLOCK

The Chinese read the time in the eyes of cats.

One day a missionary walking in a suburb of Nanking found that he had forgotten his watch, and asked a little boy what time it was.

The urchin of the Celestial Empire hesitated; then, making up his mind, he said: "I'll go and find out for you." A few seconds later he returned, holding in his arms a big cat. Looking it straight in the eye—as the phrase goes—he unhesitatingly affirmed: "It's not yet quite noon." He was right.

I myself whenever I bend down towards the lovely Felina (beautiful name!), who is at once the glory of her sex, the pride of my heart and the perfume of my soul, then always, by night or day, in broad daylight or thick darkness, deep in her adorable eyes I can distinctly read the time—always the same time, a huge and solemn hour, as vast as space, undivided into minutes or seconds; a motionless hour not marked on clocks, yet as light as a sigh, as fleeting as a glance.

And if some importunate being were to disturb me whilst my gaze rests on this delightful clock; if some rascally and intolerant Djinn, some Demon of mischance were to say to me: "At what are you looking so fixedly? What do you seek in this creature's eyes? Can you read the hour there, O prodigal and idle mortal?" I would answer without hesitation: "Yes, I can read the hour: the hour of Eternity!"

Well, that's a madrigal truly worthy of its subject—don't you agree, madam?—and as emphatic as yourself. Indeed, I have had such pleasure in elaborating this stilted compliment that I shall ask nothing of you in exchange.

XVII

A HEMISPHERE OF TRESSES

Let me go on for a long, long time breathing in the fragrance of your hair; let me bathe my whole face in it, like a thirsting man in the water of a spring; let me wave it in my hand like a scented handkerchief, to fill the air with memories.

If you could but know all that I see, feel and hear in your tresses! My soul voyages upon their perfume, as other men's souls upon music.

There is a whole dream in your hair, a dream full of sails and masts; great seas whose white crests carry me to charming climates where space is bluer and deeper, where the atmosphere is scented with fruits, leaves and human skin.

In the ocean of your hair I behold a harbour teeming with melancholy songs, lusty men of all nations, vessels of all shapes outlining their delicate and complicated structures against an immense sky on which lounges an everlasting heat.

In the caresses of your hair I recapture the languors of long hours passed on a sofa in the cabin of a handsome ship, hours lulled by the imperceptible swaying of a vessel in harbour; between pots of flowers and cool, porous water-jugs.

By the blazing hearth of your hair I breathe in the odour of tobacco mixed with opium and sugar; in the night of your hair I see the splendour of the infinite tropical azure; on the downy banks of your hair I am intoxicated by the combined odours of tar, musk and coconut oil.

Let me go on for a long time biting your heavy, dark tresses. When I gnaw at your elastic and rebellious hair, I seem to be eating my memories.

XVIII

INVITATION TO THE VOYAGE

It's a superb country, a land of Cockayne, so they say, that I dream of visiting with an old friend. An odd country, drowned in our Northern mists, a country that might be called the Orient of the Occident, the China of Europe—so

free a rein does it give to hot, capricious fancy, so patiently
and wilfully does it enrich the fancy with its cunning and
delicate vegetation.

A true land of Cockayne, where everything is beautiful,
rich, peaceful, honourable; where luxury takes pleasure in
mirroring itself in order; where life is rich and sweet to
inhale; whence disorder, turbulence and everything unforeseen are excluded; where happiness is wedded with silence;
where even the cooking is poetical, at once rich and stimulating; where everything is just like you, my angel.

You know, my dear, the feverish distress that seizes on us
amidst these chilly squalors; the yearning for an unknown
country, the agony of seeking! It is a country just like you,
where everything is beautiful, rich, peaceful and honourable,
where fancy has built and adorned an occidental China,
where life is sweet to inhale, where happiness is wedded
with silence. Thither would we fain go to live, thither would
we fain go to die!

Yes, it is thither we would fain go, to breathe, dream and
prolong the hours by the infinity of sensations. A musician
has written an "Invitation to the Valse"; who is the man who
will compose an "Invitation to the Voyage" which one can
offer to the beloved, to the sister of one's choosing?

Yes, it is in that atmosphere that life would be good—
yonder where the longer hours are richer in thoughts, where
the clocks strike the hour of happiness with deep and more
significant solemnity.

On lustrous panels, or on gilded leathers of a sombre
richness, discreetly glow paintings of a calm and deep
beatitude, like the souls of the artists who created them.
Sunsets, richly colouring the dining-room or drawing-room,
filter through gorgeous stuffs or through tall windows,
of lavish workmanship, divided by their leaden frames into
numerous sections. The furniture is huge, elaborate, strange,
equipped with locks and secret places like those of sophistica-

ted souls. The mirrors, metals, goldsmith's work and faïence entertain the eyes with a mute, mysterious symphony. From every object, every corner, every crack of a drawer or fold of stuff, exudes a singular perfume, a tantalising memory of Sumatra, which is the room's very soul.

A true land of Cockayne, as I told you, where everything is rich, clean and lustrous, like a clear conscience, like a magnificent kitchen-range, like a goldsmith's splendid creation; like a mosaic of jewels! Hither pour the world's treasures, as into the home of an industrious man who has deserved well of the entire world. A strange country, superior to others as art is to nature; a country where nature has been improved upon by dream, where nature has been corrected, beautified, recast.

By all means let them go on seeking, the alchemists of horticulture! Let them ceaselessly widen the horizons of their happiness. Let them offer prizes of sixty thousand, a hundred thousand florins to whoever will solve their ambitious problems. For my part, I have found my black tulip, my blue dahlia!

Incomparable flower, tulip rediscovered, allegorical dahlia! It is there, is it not in that lovely land of calm and fancy that you would like to live and bloom? Would you not there be framed in your own counterpart? Would you not there see yourself reflected (to speak as mystics do) in your own "affinity"?

Dreams, forever dreams! The more ambitious and delicate the soul, the more its dreams are impossible of realisation. Every man carries within himself his own dose of natural opium, incessantly secreted and renewed. Yet, from our birth to our death, how many hours can we count that have been filled with active joy, with planned and successful purpose? Shall we never live there, shall we never enter into this picture that my mind has painted—this picture that is just like you?

These treasures, furnishings, luxuries, signs of good order, perfumes, miraculous flowers, they are you. You, again, are these great rivers, these quiet canals. These huge ships that they bear along, all laden with riches and ringing with the monotonous songs of the deckhands, these are my thoughts, slumbering or travelling upon your breast. Gently you carry them towards the sea of the Infinite, meanwhile reflecting the depths of the sky in the limpidity of your lovely soul. And when, weary of the surge and crammed with the products of the Orient, they return to the homeland harbour, they are still my thoughts, grown wealthy, returning from the Infinite to you.

XIX

THE POOR CHILD'S TOY

I wish to suggest a harmless form of entertainment. There are so few amusements that are not blameworthy!

When you go out of a morning, intending to stroll along the busy streets, fill your pockets with little inventions, costing a halfpenny each—the little flat jumpingjack moved by a single piece of string, the blacksmiths hammering on their anvil, the rider and his horse whose tail is a whistle—and, at every tavern or tree you pass, pay homage with them to the poor little strangers whom you meet. You'll see their eyes widen beyond measure. At first they will not dare to take your offering; they will doubt their good fortune. Then their hands will eagerly seize the gift, and they'll run away—as a cat does when it carries off a morsel you have given it, because it has learnt to distrust human beings.

At a roadside, behind the railings of a vast garden at the end of which could be seen a pretty white country house soaked in sunlight, stood a handsome, clean little boy dressed in those country clothes that are always so attractive.

Children like this grow so handsome—as a result of luxury, freedom from care, and the accustomed spectacle of wealth—that they seem to be made of another clay than are children of moderate fortune or of poverty.

By this child's side lay on the grass a splendid toy, as clean as its owner, varnished, gilded, clad in a purple robe and covered with plumes and trinkets. But the child was paying no attention to his favourite toy; he was looking at something else.

On the other side of the railings, amongst the thistles and nettles at the road's edge, was another child, unwashed, puny, grimy, one of those pariah-brats in whom an impartial eye might discover beauty—if, like the eye of a connoisseur discovering a magnificent painting behind a coachbuilder's layer of varnish, it could clean off the revolting patina of poverty.

Through this symbolic barrier between two worlds, between the highroad and the country house, the poor child was showing the rich child the former's own toy, which the rich child was avidly examining as a rare and unknown object. This toy, which the little guttersnipe was tormenting and shaking in a cage, was a live rat! His family, to save money, no doubt, had obtained the toy from life itself.

And the two children were fraternally laughing, one to the other, with teeth of an "egalitarian" whiteness.

XXV

AN HEROIC DEATH

Fancioulle was an admirable clown, and almost one of the Prince's friends. But people assigned to the comedian's estate are always fatally attracted by serious matters; and, odd though it may appear that ideas of patriotism and liberty should take despotic hold of a Thespian's brain, one day Fancioulle entered into a conspiracy hatched by certain discontented noblemen.

The world is full of gentlemanly fellows who are ready to denounce to the ruling power those atrabilious individuals who seek to depose princes and carry out the reconstruction of a whole society without obtaining that society's leave. The noble persons in question were arrested, Fancioulle with them, and condemned irrevocably to death.

I should like to think that the Prince was almost sorry to find his favourite actor amongst the revels. The Prince was no better nor worse than another; but an excessive sensibility caused him to be, in many cases, crueller and more despotic than his peers. A passionate lover of the fine arts, and an excellent connoisseur to boot, his desire for pleasure was truly insatiable. Rather indifferent in his attitude towards people or morals, being himself a true artist, he knew no dangerous enemy but boredom; and his bizarre efforts to rout or defeat this universal tyrant would certainly have earned for him, from a severe historian, the epithet of "monster", had it been permitted in his domains to write anything at all that did not conduce solely to pleasure, or to amazement, which is one of the most delicate forms of pleasure. This Prince's great misfortune was that he never had a theatre huge enough for his genius. There are young Nero's who stifle within too narrow bounds, whose names and good intentions will always be unknown to future ages. Unforeseeing Providence had given this one faculties greater than his Estates.

Suddenly there was a rumour that the Sovereign wished to pardon all the conspirators. The origin of this rumour was an announcement of a great spectacle in which Fancioulle would play one of his principal and best rôles, and in which, it was said, even the condemned noblemen would take part: clear evidence, said superficial thinkers, of the generous inclinations of the offended Prince.

In a man both naturally and deliberately so eccentric, anything was possible, even virtue—even clemency, especially if he had been able to hope for any unexpected pleasures to be found in it. But for those who, like myself, had been able to penetrate further into the depths of this strange, sick soul, it seemed infinitely more likely that the Prince wished to gauge the scenic talents of a man under sentence of death. He wished to exploit the opportunity for a physiological experiment of truly "capital" interest, and to ascertain up to what point the habitual faculties of an actor could be changed or modified by an extraordinary situation. Did there also lurk in his soul some more or less arrested idea of clemency? This is a point upon which it has never been possible to throw light.

At last the great day came, and the little Court deployed its full ceremonial. It would be difficult to imagine, without having seen it, what the privileged class of a small State, with limited resources, can produce in the way of splendour for a really important occasion. This occasion was doubly important by reason both of the magical luxury displayed and also of its moral significance and the mystery associated with it.

Messire Fancioulle especially excelled at dumb rôles, or rôles with few words, such as are often the chief ones in legendary pieces that aim symbolically to portray the mystery of life. He came on the stage with a light step and an air of complete self-assurance: this helped to strengthen in the noble public its expectation of leniency and forgiveness.

When one says of a comedian: "He's a good actor", one implies by this expression that behind the part he plays one can still discern the actor himself—that is to say, his art, his deliberate effort. If, therefore, an actor succeeded in becoming, in relation to his part, what the best statues of antiquity would become, if miraculously given organic life and able to walk and see, in relation to the general and confused idea of beauty; why, then, that would undoubtedly be a strange and utterly unforeseen event. Fancioulle was on this evening a perfect characterisation—something that one could not help regarding as alive, possible, real. This clown came and went, laughed, wept and contorted himself, with an indestructible halo around his head—a halo, invisible to everybody but myself, which strangely combined the radiance of art and the glory of the martyr. Even into his most extravagant clownings Fancioulle introduced, by I know not what special grace, something of the divine and supernatural. My pen trembles, and the tears of an emotion that has never left me mount to my eyes, as I seek to describe for you this unforgettable evening. Fancioulle proved to me, in a peremptory and irrefutable fashion, that the intoxication of Art is the best thing of all for veiling the terrors of the Pit; that genius can play an actor's part at the edge of the tomb with a joy that prevents it from seeing the tomb—lost as it is in a paradise that excludes all notion of the tomb or of destruction.

The whole of this audience, as spoilt and frivolous as any in the world, soon fell under the artist's mighty dominion. Nobody dreamt any longer of death, grief or tortures. Every onlooker gave himself up without a care to the manifold delights to be had from the sight of a living masterpiece. Time and again explosions of joy and admiration shook the arched roof of the building with the force of a continual thunder. The Prince himself, utterly carried away, mingled his applause with that of his Court.

Nevertheless a seeing eye could discern that in him the intoxication was mingled with something else. Did he feel that he had suffered a defeat in his despotic power? A humiliation in his art of terrifying hearts and benumbing souls? A frustration of his hopes, a derision of his inward predictions? Such thoughts as these, not exactly justified, but not utterly unjustifiable, crossed my mind as I watched the Prince's face, on which a new pallor spread itself over his habitual pallor, like snow piling up on snow. Even as he ostentatiously applauded his former friend's talents, his lips became more and more tightly set, and his eyes shone with a flame resembling that of jealousy and spite. A moment came when I saw his Highness lean down to a little page standing behind him, and whisper in his ear. The pretty child's roguish face lit up with a smile, and he quickly left the Royal Box, as if on an urgent errand.

A few minutes later a shrill, long whistle interrupted Fancioulle at one of his best moments, rending all ears and hearts. From the part of the hall whence this unexpected sign of disapproval had come, a boy dashed giggling into the corridor.

Fancioulle, jerked out of his ecstatic absorption, first shut his eyes, then almost immediately opened them—immeasurably enlarged—parted his lips as if in a convulsive gasp, tottered a pace forward and a pace back, and fell stone dead on the boards.

Was it really the whistle, as swift as the blade of a sword, that had cheated the executioner? Had the Prince himself guessed the full murderous efficacity of his ruse? It is permissible to suspect it. Did he regret the loss of his dear and inimitable Fancioulle? It is clement and legitimate to believe it.

The guilty noblemen had acted in their last play. That same night they were erased from life.

Since then many actors justly appreciated in their own countries have come to play at the Court of . . . . . ; but none of them has been able to remind one of Fancioulle's marvellous gifts, or to attain the same height of "Royal favour".

XXXIII

BE YOU DRUNKEN!

One must always be drunk. That's all there is to it; that's the only solution. In order not to feel the horrible burden of Time breaking your shoulders and bowing your head to the ground, you must be drunken without respite.

But with what? With wine, poetry or virtue, as you will. Be you drunken.

And if sometimes you awake, on the steps of a palace, in the green herbage of a ditch or in the dreary solitude of your room, then ask the wind, the waves, the stars, the birds, the clocks, ask everything that runs, that moans, that moves on wheels, everything that sings and speaks—ask them what is the time of day; and the wind, the waves, the stars, the birds and the clocks will answer you: "It is time to get drunk. In order not to be the martyred slave of Time, be you drunken; be you drunken ceaselessly! With wine, poetry or virtue, as you will."

XXXIV

ALREADY

A hundred times already the sun had burst forth, radiant or sorrowful, from this huge vat of a sea whose horizon can scarcely be seen; a hundred times it had plunged again, sparkling or morose, in its huge evening bath. For several days we had been able to contemplate the other side of the firmament and decipher the celestial alphabet of the Antipodes. And each of the passengers groaned and grumbled. One would have thought that the approach of land exacerbated their suffering. "When," they said, "shall we stop having our sleep shaken by the swell and troubled by a wind that snores louder than we do? When shall we be able to digest our meals in a motionless armchair?"

There were some who thought of home, longing for their unfaithful and cantankerous wives and their squalling progenies. All were so crazed by the mental picture of vanished land that I think they could have eaten grass more eagerly than animals.

At last the sight of a shore was reported; and we saw, as we approached it, that this was a magnificent, a dazzling land. The melodies of life seemed to pour from it in a vague murmur, and its coasts, rich in all sorts of greenery, seemed to exhale to a distance of several leagues a delicious odour of flowers and fruit.

At once everyone was joyful, everyone cast off his ill humour. All quarrels were forgotten, all mutual wrongs forgiven; the duels that had been arranged were erased from memory; rancours melted away like puffs of smoke.

I alone was sad, unconceivably sad. Like a priest deprived of his Divinity, it was only with a harrowing sense of bitterness that I could tear myself from this sea, so monstrously seductive, so infinitely varied in its terrifying simplicity; this sea which seems to contain within itself, its behaviour, its rages and smiles, all the moods, agonies and ecstasies of all the souls that have ever lived, are living or will live.

As I bade farewell to this incomparable beauty, I felt stricken unto death; and that is why, whilst each of my companions was saying: "At last!" I could only exclaim: "Already!"

Nevertheless, it was land—land with its noises, its passions, its commodities, its festivals; it was a rich and magnificent land, full of promise, that was sending out to us a mysterious scent of rose and musk, a land whence the melodies of life reached us in an amorous murmur.

XXXV

WINDOWS

A man who looks out of an open window never sees as much as a man who looks at a window that is shut. There is nothing deeper, more mysterious, more fertile, more murky or more dazzling than a window lit by a candle. What one can see in the light of day is always less interesting than what happens behind a pane of glass. In this black or lustrous pit lives life. Here life dreams, life suffers.

Beyond the wave-crests of the roofs I see a woman of mature age, already wrinkled, a poor woman who always stoops over something and never goes out. From her face, clothes and movements—from almost nothing at all—I have recreated this woman's story, or her legend, rather; and sometimes I narrate it to myself, weeping.

If it had been a poor old man, I would have recreated his legend just as easily.

And I go to bed, proud of having lived and suffered in others but myself.

Perhaps you will say to me: "Are you sure that your legend is true?" How does it matter what the reality outside of myself may be, if it has helped me to live, and to feel that I am, and what I am?

XXXIX

A BLOOD MARE

She is quite ugly—and yet she is delightful! Time and Love have marked her with their claws, and have cruelly taught her how much youth and freshness every minute and every kiss take away.

She is truly ugly; she is an ant, a spider, if you like, even a skeleton; but she is also a potion, a magistery, a witchcraft! In short, she is exquisite!

Time has not been able to break the gently sparkling harmony of her gait, or the indestructible elegance of her frame. Love has not altered the suavity of her childish breath; nor has Time snatched away any of her abundant mane, in whose wild scents breathes all the devilish vitality of the French South: Nîmes, Aix, Arles, Avignon, Narbonne, Toulouse—towns blessed by the sun, amorous and charming!

Time and Love have gnawed in vain at her lovely teeth; they have diminished none of the vague but eternal charm of her boyish breast.

Worn out, perhaps, but not fatigued, and always heroic, she reminds one of those horses of the finest bloodstock whom the eye of a true connoisseur can recognise even between the shafts of a hackney-carriage or a heavy waggon.

Besides, she is so gentle and so hotly loving! She makes love as people do in autumn; the approach of winter seems to kindle a new fire in her heart; and in the servility of her tenderness there is nothing wearisome.

XLI

THE HARBOUR

A harbour is a charming retreat for a soul weary of life's struggles. The breath of the sky, the shifting architecture of the clouds, the changing hues of the sea, the scintillation of lighthouses, are a prism marvellously adapted to entertain the eyes without ever fatiguing them. The slender shapes of the vessels with their complicated riggings, vessels to which the surf imparts harmonious oscillations, help to foster in the soul the taste for rhythm and beauty. Moreover, there is a kind of mysterious and aristocratic pleasure, for a man who has no more curiosity or ambition, in lying in the belvedere, or resting his elbows on the mole and contemplating all those movements of people departing and returning—people who still have the strength of wishing, of the desire to travel or grow wealthy.

XLIV

SOUP AND CLOUDS

My crazy little belovèd was giving me dinner, and through the open window of the dining-room I was gazing at the shifting architecture that God creates with vapours, the marvellous structures of the impalpable. And I was thinking to myself, in the midst of my gazing: "All these fantasmagorias are almost as beautiful as the eyes of my beautiful belovéd—the crazy little monster with the green eyes."

And suddenly I was struck a violent blow in the back, and I heard a husky and charming voice, a voice hysterical and as if thickened by brandy, saying to me: "Are you or aren't you going to eat your soup, you bloody old cloud-merchant?"

XLVI

A LOST HALO

"Hallo, what, you here, my dear fellow? You, in a place of ill fame! You, the drinker of quintessences, the eater of ambrosia! Really, I *am* surprised!"

"My dear fellow, you know how I have a horror of horses and carriages. Just now, as I was crossing the boulevard, in a great hurry, skipping through the mud, amidst all that moving chaos in which death comes galloping at you from all sides at once, suddenly my halo slipped off my head into the mire on the macadam. I hadn't the courage to pick it up. I decided that it was less disagreeable to lose my insignia of rank than to have my bones broken. Besides, I said to myself, every misfortune has its advantage. Now I can go about incognito, commit base actions, indulge in debauch, like ordinary mortals. So here I am, looking just like you, as you see!"

"You ought to advertise for the halo, or report its loss to the police-station."

"I certainly shall not. I'm enjoying myself here. You're the only person who has recognised me. Besides, dignity bores me. Furthermore, there's the joyful thought that some bad poet will pick it up and impudently put it on. It's such a delight to make somebody happy—especially somebody who will look ridiculous in his happiness. Think of X wearing it, or Z! Won't that be funny?"

XLVIII

ANYWHERE OUT OF THE WORLD[1]

Life is a hospital in which every patient is possessed by a desire to change his bed. This man wants to be ill in front of the stove, that man thinks he would get well by the window.

It always seems to me that I'd be better off somewhere else, and this question of changing my place of abode is one that I continually discuss with my soul.

"Tell me, soul—you poor, chilled soul—what would you say to living in Lisbon? It must be warm there, and you could frisk like a lizard. The city's at the water's edge. People say that it's built of marble, and that the inhabitants have such

1 In English and French in the original.

a hatred of anything vegetable that they uproot all the trees. That's a landscape to your taste—a landscape made of light and minerals, with liquid to mirror them!"

My soul does not reply.

"Since you're so fond of repose accompanied by the spectacle of movement, would you like to come and live in Holland, that land of beatitude? Perhaps you'd find entertainment in that country, whose image you have so often admired in museums? What would you say to Rotterdam— you who are so fond of forests of masts, and ships moored below houses?"

My soul is still mute.

"Perhaps Batavia would attract you more? We'd find there the mind of Europe married to the beauty of the tropics."

Not a word. Can my soul be dead?

"Have you then, reached such a point of numbness that you can take pleasure only in your misfortune? If so, let us flee to the countries that are analogies of Death . . . . I know what we'll do, my poor soul! We'll pack our trunks for Tornio. Let's go even further—right to the far end of the Baltic; even further away from life than that, if we can: let's instal ourselves at the Pole. That's where the sun brushes the earth only obliquely, and the slow alternations of light and night suppress variety and enhance monotony— which is half of nothingness. We'll be able to take long baths of darkness; not but what the aurora borealis will from time to time offer, for our diversion, its rosy wreaths like reflections of Hell's fireworks!"

At last my soul explodes, sagaciously exclaiming: "Any-where, anywhere, out of the world!"

JOURNALS AND NOTEBOOK

JOURNALS AND NOTEBOOK

ROCKETS

I

Even if God did not exist, religion would still be holy and divine.

God is the only being who, in order to rule, does not need even to exist.

Creations of the mind are more alive than matter.

Love is a liking for prostitution. There are no pleasures, not even noble ones, whose origin cannot be traced to prostitution.

At a theatre or ball, each person is being pleasured by everybody else.

What is art? Prostitution.

The pleasure of being in a crowd is a mysterious expression of delight in the multiplication of number. Number is *all*, and in all. Number is within the individual. Intoxication is a number.

In a man who has reached maturity, the taste for ruinous dispersal should be replaced by a taste for productive concentration.

Love may arise from a generous sentiment—namely, the liking for prostitution; but it soon becomes corrupted by the liking for ownership.

Love seeks to escape from itself, to mingle itself with its victim, as a victor nation with the vanquished—and yet at the same time to retain the privileges of a conqueror.

The sensual pleasures of a man who keeps a mistress have

in them something both of the angel and of the proprietor. Charity and ferocity. They are even independent of sex, of beauty and of animality.

Green shadows on damp evenings in summer.

The immense profundity of thought contained in common-place turns of phrase—holes burrowed by generations of ants.

The story of the Hunter, as an illustration of the intimate connection between love and ferocity.

II

Rockets: On the feminity of the Church as the reason of its omnipotence.

On the colour violet (inhibited love, love veiled and mysterious, the colour of canonesses).

The priest is immense because he creates belief in a multitude of amazing things.

It is a law of human nature that the Church should wish to do everything and be everything.

Peoples worship authority.

Priests are the servants and votaries of the imagination.

Throne and altar, a revolutionary maxim.

E.G., or the Seducer-Adventuress.

Religious intoxication of great cities.

Pantheism: I am all; all are I.

Maelstrom.

III

Rockets: I think I've already written, in one of my notes, that love is very like a torture or a surgical operation. But this idea can be still more bitterly expressed. Even though a pair of lovers may be deeply devoted, full of mutual desires, one of them will always be calmer, or less obsessed, than the other. He or she must be the surgeon or torturer; the other the patient or victim.

Do you hear those sighs, preludes to a tragedy of shame, those moans, those screams, those rattles in the throat? Who has not uttered them, who has not irresistibly extorted them? What makes you consider that "the question" applied by skilled torturers is in any way worse? Those somnambulist's eyes, rolled back to show their whites; those limbs whose muscles jerk and stiffen as if under the action of an electric battery; not intoxication, madness or opium, even in their most raging manifestations, will ever offer you such appalling and interesting symptoms. And the human face—which Ovid thought was made to mirror the stars— see it now, no longer expressing anything but a crazy ferocity, or rigid in a kind of death! Indeed, I should think it blasphemy to apply the word "ecstasy" to this kind of collapse into rottenness.

Dreadful game, in which one of the players must lose his or her self-government!

The question was once asked in my presence, in what did love's greatest pleasure consist? Of course somebody answered "in receiving", another "in giving", a third "in the pleasure of pride" and a fourth "in the sensual thrill of humility." All these obscene creatures were talking like the *Imitatio Christi*. There was even one impudent Utopist who asserted that the greatest pleasure of love-making was to create citizens for the fatherland!

For my part, I say that the unique and supreme pleasure in love-making lies in the certain knowledge that one is doing *evil*. Men and women know from birth that in evil lies all pleasure of the sense.

IV

Plans. Rockets. Projects: Play at the Silvestre. Barbora and the sheep.

Chenavard has created a superhuman character.

My vow to Levaillant.

Preface a mixture of mysticality and playfulness.

Dreams, and theories concerning dreams, in the style of Swedenborg.

Campbell's view (the Conduct of Life).

Concentration.

Power of the preconceived idea.

Absolute frankness, a means to originality.

Telling funny stories with a pompous expression.

V

Rockets. Notes: When a man takes to his bed, almost all his friends secretly hope to see him die: some to prove that his health was inferior to theirs; others in a disinterested wish to study an agony.

The arabesque is the most spiritual of designs.

VI

Rockets. Notes: The man of letters invests and re-invests his funds, and thus creates a liking for intellectual gymnastics.

The arabesque is the most ideal of designs.

We love women in proportion to their degree of strangeness to us.

To love intelligent women is a paederast's pleasure. Thus bestiality and paederasty are mutually exclusive.

The spirit of buffoonery may, in some cases, not exclude charity—but very seldom.

Enthusiasm for anything other than abstractions is a sign of weakness and sickness.

A thin body is more naked, more indecent than a fat one.

VII

Tragic heaven: Abstract epithet applied to a material being.

Man drinks in light along with the atmosphere. That is why people are right in saying that night air is unhealthy for work.

The populace are born fire-worshippers.

Fireworks, arson, incendiaries.

By imagining a born fire-worshipper, a born Parsee, one can create a new. . .

VIII

Feelings of contempt for other people's faces are the result of an eclipse of the actual image by the hallucination that arises from it.

Learn, therefore, the joys of an austere life, and pray, pray ceaselessly. Prayer is a reservoir of strength. (Altar of the Will. Moral dynamic. The Sorcery of the Sacraments. Hygiene of the Soul.)

Music fathoms the sky.

Jean-Jacques said that he never entered a café without a certain emotion. For a shy nature, the box-office of a theatre slightly resembles the tribunal of Hell.

Life has only one real charm—the charm of *gambling*. But what if we do not care whether we win or lose?

IX

Notes. Rockets: Nations have great men only despite themselves—just like families. They make every effort not to have them. This means that a great man, in order to exist, must have a power of attack greater than the power of resistance developed by millions of individuals.

On the subject of sleep, that sinister adventure upon which we embark every night, it can be said that men daily fall asleep with an audacity that would be incomprehensible if we did not know it to result from ignorance of the danger.

X

There are certain elephants' hides against which disdain ceases to be a vengeance.

The more friends you have, the more gloves you need. Those who have been my friends were people of no repute—disreputable people, I should even say, if I had any wish to flatter the reputable.

Girardin talking Latin! *Pescudesque locutae*.

He belonged to a Society of unbelievers, whose object was to send Robert Houdin amongst the Arabs, to discourage their belief in miracles.

XI

These great, handsome ships, imperceptibly swaying—cradled, so to speak—upon the tranquil waters; these sturdy ships, with their air of idleness and nostalgia, surely they dumbly ask us: "When do we set sail for happiness?"

Mem.: The miraculous aspect of drama, its sorcery and romanticism.

The feeling of circumstance and atmosphere in which any tale should be soaked. (Compare *Usher*, and relate to the profound sensations caused by hashish and opium.)

XII

Can there be madness in mathematics? Are there crazy people who think that two and two make three? In other terms, can hallucination—if only these words do not shriek aloud, at being coupled together!—can hallucination invade the spheres of pure reason?

If, when a man has acquired the habit of idleness, day-dreaming and loafing, to such a degree that he ceaselessly puts off everything of importance until tomorrow—if, then, some other man were one morning to awaken him with heavy strokes of a whip, and were pitilessly to whip him until he, who could not work for pleasure, must work for very fear; would not our second man—the man with the whip—really be the friend and benefactor of the first?

One can at least say: "The pleasure comes afterwards"—a far more accurate statement than: "Love comes after marriage."

In politics, similarly, the true saint is the man who whips and kills the people, for the people's good.

Thursday, May 13th, 1856.

Get copies from Michel.

Write to Moun,

to Urriès,

to Maria Clemm.

Send to Mrs. Dumay to know if Mirès . . . .

Anything that is not slightly misshapen has an air of insensibility.

Hence it follows that irregularity—that is to say, the unexpected, surprise, astonishment—is an essential part, and, indeed, *the* characteristic, of beauty.

XIII

Notes. Rockets: Theodore de Banville is not exactly a materialist; he is luminous.

His poetry is an account of hours of happiness.

In answer to every letter from a creditor write fifty lines on an extra-terrestrial subject, and you'll be saved.

A beaming smile spreads over the handsome ogre's face.

"On suicide and suicide-whilst-of-unsound-mind, considered under their statistical, medical and philosophical aspects."

Brierre de Boismont.

Look up the passage: *"Living with a person who feels nothing for you but aversion . . . . "*

Seneca's portrait of "Serenus." The portrait of Stagirus by St. John Chrysostom. *Accidie*, malady of monks.

Taedium vitae. . . .

XV

Rockets: Interpretation and paraphrase of *Love conquers all*.

Spiritual and physical delights caused by storms, electricity and lightning—tocsin of darkling, amorous memories of years gone by.

XVI

Rockets: I have discovered the definition of Beauty—of *my* Beauty.

It is something ardent and sad, something slightly vague, giving rein to conjecture.

I shall, if you wish, apply my ideas to a perceptible object; to the most interesting object to be found in society for example, namely, to a woman's face. A lovely and enticing face—a woman's face, I mean—is something that makes you dream simultaneously but confusedly of sensual pleasure and of sorrow. It conveys an idea of melancholy, of weariness, even of satiety—and at the same time a contrary idea: an ardour, a desire to live, coupled with a recurrent bitterness, such as might come of privation or despair. Mystery and regret, too, are characteristics of Beauty.

A handsome *male* face, on the other hand, does not need to convey the suggestion of sensual pleasure (to a male beholder, I mean, of course—a woman may think otherwise): that suggestion which, when conveyed by a woman's face, is all the more provocative in that the face itself is, as a rule, the more melancholy because of it.

Such a face (a male one) will, however, have something ardent and sad—spiritual yearnings—ambitions darkly suppressed—the notion of force seething in idleness—sometimes the notion of a revengeful indifference (for we must not, when considering this subject, forget the ideal type of Dandy).

Sometimes, too—and this is one of the most interesting characteristics of beauty—it will have mystery; and lastly (let me have the courage to admit how modern I feel myself to be in matters of aesthetics), it will have *unhappiness*.

I do not claim that Joy cannot associate with Beauty; but I say that Joy is one of Beauty's most vulgar adornments, whereas Melancholy is, so to speak, her illustrious companion —so much so that I can scarcely imagine (is my brain a mirror bewitched?) a type of Beauty in which there is no *Unhappiness*.

Supporting my reasoning upon these ideas—or, as other people would say, obsessed with them—it is obviously difficult for me to avoid the conclusion that the most perfect type of male beauty is *Satan* as depicted by Milton.

XVII

Rockets: Auto-idolatry. / Poetic harmony of character. / Eurhythmics of character and faculties. / Need to conserve all faculties. / Enhance all faculties.

Study of a cult (magism, conjurative sorcery). Sacrifice and the taken vow are the supreme formulas, and the symbols of exchange.

Two basic literary qualities: superrealism and irony. An individual way of seeing things—the aspect under which things present themselves to the writer; also a satanic turn of mind. The supernatural comprises colour in general, and also accent—that is to say, intensity, sonority, lucidity, vibration, depth and resonance in space and time.

There are moments of existence when time and expanse are more profound, and the sense of existence is hugely enhanced.

On magic applied to the conjuration of the mighty dead, and to the regaining and perfecting of health.

Inspiration always comes when a man wishes; but it does not always go when he wishes.

On language and writing as magical functions, conjurative sorcery.

On Woman's airs :

The airs that have charm, and that constitute beauty, are:

The air of sophisticated weariness,

The air of boredom,

The swooning air,

The impudent air,

The chilly air,
The air of looking down from a height,
The air of domination,
The air of wilfulness,
The air of malignity,
The air of sickness,
The air of a pussy-cat—a mixture of childishness, non-chalance and malice.

In certain almost supernatural states of the soul, the profundity of life is entirely revealed in any scene, however ordinary, that presents itself before one. The scene becomes its Symbol.

As I was crossing the Boulevard, hurrying a little to avoid the carriages, my halo was shaken loose and fell into the mud on the macadam. I luckily had time to pick it up; but a moment later this unfortunate notion crept into my mind —which was a bad omen. And since then the notion will not leave me alone; it has given me no peace all day.

On the cult of oneself in love—from the point of view of health, hygiene, care of the person, spiritual nobility and eloquence.

Self-purification and anti-humanity[1]

There is in the act of love a great resemblance to torture, or to a surgical operation.

There is in prayer a certain use of magic. Prayer is one of the great forces of the intellectual dynamic. It plays the part of a current of electricity.

The rosary is a medium, a vehicle; it is prayer put at everybody's disposal.

Work as a progressive and accumulative force, bearing interest as financial capital does, both in the faculties themselves and in their results.

Mere amateur activity, even if controlled by science, which is but an intermittent force, will always, and however

1 In English in the original.

fruitful it may be, take second place to work, however slight, provided work be continuous.

If a poet demanded from the State the right to keep a few bourgeois in his stable, people would be very surprised; whereas, if a bourgeois demanded a roast poet, people would find this quite natural.

This fact cannot possibly scandalise the women of my household, my mistresses or my sisters.

Sometimes he used to ask her leave for him to kiss her leg; and he would profit by the occasion to kiss that lovely limb in such a position that its contours were clearly outlined against the sunset!

"*Minette, minouette, minouille*, my pussy, my wolf, my little chimpanzee, you big baboon, you big snake, my gloomy little chimpanzee."

Such verbal whimsicalities as these, too many times repeated—animal nicknames used far too often—are evidence of a satanic side to love. Are not devils shaped like animals? Remember Cazotte's camel—camel, devil and woman.

A man goes out pistol-shooting, accompanied by his wife. He sets up a popinjay, and says to his wife: "I'm imagining that it's you."

He shuts his eyes, and knocks down the popinjay.

Then he kisses his companion's hand, and says: "Angel, thank you so much for helping me to shoot so straight!"

By the time when I shall have succeeded in inspiring universal disgust and horror, I shall have gained solitude.

This book is not written for the women of my household, my mistresses or my sisters—I have few of any of these chattels.

There are certain elephants' hides against which disdain ceases to be a pleasure.

The more friends you have, the more gloves you need—for fear of the itch.

Those who have been my friends were people of no repute
—disreputable people, I should even say, if I had any wish
to flatter the reputable.

God is a scandal—a scandal that spreads.

XVIII

Rockets: Never despise any person's sensibility. His
sensibility is his genius.

There are only two places in which one pays for the right
of giving something away: public lavatories and brothels.

An enthusiastic "life in sin" can give one a glimpse of the
delights of a young married couple.

On precocious love of women: I used to mistake the smell
of fur for the smell of woman. I can remember how . . . .
When all is said, what I loved my mother for was her elegance.
In other words, I was a precocious Dandy.

My ancestors, idiots or maniacs, in their stately dwellings
—all of them victims of appalling passions.

Protestant countries lack two elements that are indispensable to the well-being of a man of breeding: gallantry
and devotion.

A mixture of the grotesque and the tragic is agreeable to
the intellect, just as discords are agreeable to sophisticated
ears.

The intoxicating thing about bad taste is the aristocratic
pleasure in giving offence.

Germany expresses its daydreams in line, whereas England
does so in perspective.

Every engenderment of a sublime thought entails a
nervous shock, which can be felt in the cerebellum.

Spain infuses religion with the natural ferocity of love.

Style: The eternal tone, style eternal and cosmopolitan.
Chateaubriand, Alph. Rabbe, Edgar Poe.

XIX

Rockets. Suggestions It's easy to guess why democrats don't like cats. The cat is good-looking; he reveals ideas of luxury, cleanliness, physical pleasure, etc. . . .

XX

Rockets: A little work, repeated three hundred and sixty-five times, produces three hundred and sixty-five times a little money—that is to say, a huge sum. *Meanwhile, fame is won.*

In the same way, a multitude of small delights constitute happiness.

To create a new commonplace, that's genius. I must create a commonplace.

The *concetto* is a masterpiece.

The tone of Alphonse Rabbe.

The tone of the kept mistress. (*My wholly adorable! Fickle sex!*)

The eternal tone.

Crude coloration, design deeply incised

The prima donna and the butcher's-boy.

My mother is a fantasist. One must fear her and seek to please her.

The pride of Hildebrand.

Napoleon III's Caesarism. (Letter to Edgar Ney.) Pope and Emperor.

XXI

Rockets. Suggestions: Delivering oneself to Satan, what it means.

What is more absurd than Progress—seeing that man, as day-by-day events prove, is always like and equal to man: that is to say, always in a state of savagery? What are the perils of jungle and prairie compared to the daily shocks and conflicts of civilisation? Whether a man embraces his dupe on the boulevard, or spears his prey in unknown forests, is he not eternal man—that is to say, the most highly perfected beast of prey?

I'm supposed to be thirty years old; but, if I have lived three minutes in one—am I not ninety?

. . Work is surely the salt that preserves mummified souls?

How to start on a novel. Begin on any subject, no matter what. Then, in order to create a desire to finish the work, start with some particularly gorgeous phrases.

XXII

Rockets: I think that the infinite and mysterious charm that lies in the contemplation of a ship, and especially of a moving ship, is derived, in the case of a ship at anchor, from its regularity and symmetry—which are amongst the primordial needs of the human soul; and, in the case of a ship at sea, from the continual multiplication and generation of all the imaginary curves and figures produced in space by the object's real elements.

The poetic idea that arises from this process of linear movement is the notion of a huge creature, complicated but rhythmical, an animal full of genius, suffering and sighing with all the sighs and ambitions of mankind.

You civilised peoples, who always speak so stupidly of "savages" and "barbarians": there will come a time when, as D'Aurevilly says, you "won't be good enough to be idolaters."

Stoicism, the religion with only one sacrament: suicide!

Conceive of a vault for a lyrical or elfin farce or pantomime, and translate this into a serious novel. Steep the whole in an abnormal, dreamy atmosphere—in the atmosphere of "the great days of old." Let there be something *lulling* about it—even a sort of serenity found in passion. . . . Regions of pure Poetry.

Moved by contact with those pleasures of the senses that resemble memories; moved by the thought of an ill-spent past, so many faults, so many quarrels, so many things to be hidden from one another, he began to weep; and his hot tears ran, in the darkness, down the naked shoulder of his beloved and always alluring mistress. She quivered, feeling —she, too—touched and moved. The darkness consoled her vanity and her frigid woman's dandyism. These two creatures —fallen, but still afflicted by the remains of their lost nobility—spontaneously embraced; mingling, in the rain of their tears and kisses, the sorrows of their past with their very uncertain hopes of the future. It may be presumed that never, for them, was sensual pleasure so sweet as on this night of melancholy and charity—a pleasure saturated with grief and remorse.

In the blackness of the night, he had looked back over his shoulder into the depths of the years; and had then cast himself into the arms of his guilty lover, to find there for himself the forgiveness that he granted her.

Hugo often thinks of Prometheus. He applies an imaginary vulture to a breast that, in fact, is stabbed only by the hot-poultices of vanity. Then, as the hallucination progresses, taking various forms but following the course foretold by the physicians, he believes that, by a *fiat* of Providence, St. Helena has been transferred to Jersey.

The man is so un-elegiac, so unethereal, he'd make a notary shudder.

Hugo, that sacred calling, always carries his head bowed— bowed so low that he can see nothing but his nombril.

. . . . What *isn't* a sacred calling nowadays? Youth itself is a sacred calling—or so say the young.

And what *isn't* a prayer? To s—— is to pray—or so say democrats, when they're s——ing.

M. de Pontmartin—a man who always looks as if he'd just come up from one of the provinces.

Man—that is to say, everybody—is so *naturally* depraved that he suffers less from an all-round lowering of standards than he would suffer from the establishment of a reasonable hierarchy.

The world is about to come to an end. The only reason why it should continue is that it exists. What a weak argument, compared with all the arguments to the contrary, and especially the following: "What, in future, is the world to do in the sight of heaven?" For, supposing it continued to have material existence, would this existence be worthy of the name, or of the Encyclopaedia of history?

I do not say that the world will be reduced to the expedients and grotesque disorder of the South American republics; or that perhaps we may even return to a state of savagery, and prowl, gun in hand, in search of food, through the grass-covered ruins of our civilisation. No, for such adventures would imply the survival of a sort of vital energy, an echo of earlier ages. Typical victims of the inexorable moral laws, we shall perish by the thing by which we thought to live. Machinery will have so much Americanised us, progress will have so much atrophied our spiritual element, that nothing in the sanguinary, blasphemous or unnatural dreams of the Utopists can be compared to what will actually happen.

I ask any thinking man to show me what now exists of life. As for religion, I deem it useless to speak of it, or to seek for any remains of it, since in such matters the only thing that can nowadays give scandal is to take the trouble to deny God.

Property virtually disappeared with the abolition of the law of primogeniture; but a time will come when humanity, like an avenging ogre, will snatch their last morsel from those who regard themselves as legitimate heirs to the revolutions. And even that will not be the supreme disaster.

The human imagination can conceive, without too much difficulty, of republics or other communal States that would not be entirely without dignity, provided they were controlled by men of sacred vocation, by certain types of aristocrat. But it is not its political institutions that will especially characterise the universal ruin or universal progress—it matters little what name it is given. The essential characteristic will be the cheapening of hearts.

Need I add that any meagre political forces remaining will have to struggle painfully within the bonds of general animality, and that rulers will be compelled, in order to maintain themselves and to create a ghost of order, to resort to methods that would appal present-day mankind, hardened though it be?

When that time comes, the son will desert his family, not at the age of eighteen, as at present, but at the age of twelve, emancipated by his gluttonous precocity; he will run away, not in search of heroic adventures, not to deliver a beautiful prisoner from a tower, not to immortalise a garret with his sublime thoughts; but to start a business, to grow rich, to enter into competition with his vile papa, founder and chief shareholder of a journal that will spread enlightenment and make the one-time *Siècle* seem like a pillar of superstition.

When that time comes, women runagates, women who forsake their station in life—women who have had lovers, and are sometimes known as "Angels", in grateful recognition of the recklessness that shines like a will-o'-the-wisp in their existence as logical as it is evil—such women, I say, will have given place to a pitiless righteousness, a righteousness that will condemn everything except money—everything, *even errors of the senses!*

When that time comes, anything that resembles virtue—nay, anything other than ardent devotion to Plutus—will be regarded as vastly ridiculous. Justice—if, in this fortunate epoch, any justice can still exist—will forbid the existence of citizens who are unable to make their fortunes.

Your wife, O Bourgeois, your chaste other half, whose legitimacy is your poetry, giving to legality an irreproachable infamy, vigilant and loving guardian of your strongbox—your wife will be nothing more than the ideal type of kept woman. Your daughter, in her childish nubility, will dream in her cradle that she is selling herself for a million. And you yourself, O Bourgeois—even less a poet than you are today—will make no objection; you will have no complaint.

For there are things in man that thrive and prosper to the extent that other things ail and shrink; and, thanks to the "progress" of those future times, all that will be left of your bowels will be your guts!

Those times are perhaps quite close at hand. Who knows whether they are not here already; whether it is not simply the coarsening of our natures that prevents us from perceiving the atmosphere that we already breathe?

For my part, I who sometimes feel myself cast in the ridiculous role of prophet, I know that I shall never receive so much as a doctor's charity. Lost in this base world, jostled by the mob, I am like a weary man who sees behind him, in the depths of the years, only disillusionment and bitterness, and in front of him only a tempest that brings nothing new—neither instruction nor grief.

On some evening when this man has stolen from destiny a few hours of pleasure—soothed by the processes of his digestion, forgetful (so far as possible) of the past, content with the present and resigned to the future, intoxicated by his own indifference and dandyism, proud of being less base than the passers-by—he contemplates the smoke of his cigarette, and says to himself: "What care I where all these scruples go?"

I seem to have wandered off into what people of my trade call an *hors-d'oeuvre*. Nevertheless, I shall let these pages stand—because I wish to set an exact date to my anger.

MY HEART LAID BARE

I

The distillation and centralisation of the *ego*. Everything is in that.

A certain sensual enjoyment in the company of the extravagant.

(I intend to begin *My heart laid bare* at no particular place and in no particular fashion; and to continue it from day to day, following the inspiration of the day and the circumstance; provided only that the inspiration be a living one.)

II

Anybody at all has the right to talk about himself—provided he knows how to be entertaining.

III

I realise that one's object in deserting a cause is to know what it feels like to serve another cause.

It might perhaps be pleasant to be alternately victim and executioner.

IV

Stupidities by Girardin:

"It is our custom to take the bull by the horns. So let us

begin this discourse at the end."

(November 17th, 1863)

So Girardin thinks that a bull's horns grow on its rump. He confuses the horns with the tail.

"I hope that, before imitating the Ptolemies of French journalism, Belgian journalists will take the trouble to meditate on a question that I have been studying for thirty years—as will be demonstrated by a volume that will shortly be published under the title: *'Questions concerning the Press'*; and that they will not be in too great a hurry to treat as sovereignly ridiculous an opinion that is as true as is the fact that the earth turns and the sun does not."

EMILE DE GIRARDIN

V

Woman is the opposite of the Dandy. That is why she should be regarded with disgust.

Woman is hungry, and she wants to eat; thirsty, and she wants to drink.

She feels randy, and she wants to be ——.

Fine characteristics!

Woman is "natural"—that is to say, abominable.

Moreover, she is always vulgar—that is to say, the opposite of the Dandy.

Concerning the Legion of Honour: A person who applies for the Cross seems to say: "If I am not decorated for having done my duty, I shall cease to do it."

If a man has merit, what is the use of decorating him? If he has none, he may be decorated, because this will give him a certain lustre.

To consent to be decorated is to recognise the right of the State or Prince to judge you, to make you illustrious, etc.

In any case, even if pride does not do so, Christian humility forbids acceptance of this decoration.

Argument in favour of God's existence: Nothing exists without a purpose.

Therefore my existence has a purpose.

What purpose? I do not know.

It is not I who defined this purpose. It must therefore have been somebody with greater knowledge than mine.

So I must pray to this somebody to enlighten me. That's the most sensible thing to do.

The Dandy should aspire to be sublime, continually. He should live and sleep in front of a mirror.

VI

Study of the counter-religions: example, sacred prostitution.

Sacred prostitution, its meaning.

Nervous excitation.

Mysticity of paganism. Mysticism, the hyphen between paganism and Christianity.

Paganism and Christianity mutually confirm each other.

Revolution and the cult of Reason confirm the idea of sacrifice.

Superstition is the reservoir of all truths.

VII

In every change there is something at once vile and agreeable: some element of disloyalty and restlessness. This sufficiently explains the French Revolution.

VIII

My intoxication in 1848:

The nature of this intoxication. Liking for vengeance.

Natural pleasure in destruction. Literary intoxication—something remembered from books.

The fifteenth of May. Always that liking for destruction. A legitimate liking, if whatever is natural is legitimate.

The horrors of June. A madness of the masses, and a madness of the bourgeoisie. Natural love of crime.

My rage at the coup d'Etat. To how many bullets I exposed myself! Another Bonaparte! What a disgrace!

What is Emperor Napoleon III? What is he good for? Find the explanation of his nature, and of his preordained purpose.

IX

Usefulness to the community has always seemed to me a most hideous thing in a man.

1848 was amusing only because everybody was building Utopias, like castles in Spain.

1848 was charming only by reason of the very excess of its absurdity.

Robespierre's only claim to esteem is that he coined a few fine phrases.

X

Revolution, by the blood-sacrifices it performs, reinforces superstition.

XI

Politics: I have no convictions, as such things are understood by my contemporaries, because I have no ambition.

I have within myself no basis for any conviction.

There is a certain cowardice, or rather a certain softness, in respectable people.

The only men who have any conviction are brigands. Of what are they convinced? That it is necessary for them to be successful. So they *are* successful.

Why should I be successful, seeing that I have not even any wish to try to be?

Glorious empires can be founded on crime, and noble religions upon imposture.

Nevertheless, I have some convictions, but of a higher order, such as my contemporaries cannot understand.

XII

A sense of solitude, since my childhood. Despite my family, and especially amidst companions—a sense of an eternally lonely destiny.

Nevertheless, a most vivid liking for life and pleasure.

XIII

Almost our whole lives are spent in .satisfying foolish curiosities. On the other hand, there are things that ought to provoke men's curiosity to the highest degree—and yet, to judge by the tenor of men's normal lives, inspire them with no curiosity whatsoever.

Where are our friends who have died?

Why are we here?

Do we come from somewhere?

What is freedom?

Can it be reconciled with the law of predestination?

The number of souls, is it finite or infinite?

And the number of inhabitable countries?

Etc., etc.

XIV

Nations have great men only despite themselves. Therefore, the great man is the conqueror of his entire nation.

Ridiculous modern religions:

Molière,

Béranger,

Garibaldi.

XV

Belief in progress is a lazy man's creed, a creed for Belgians.

It is the individual counting on his neighbours to perform his task for him.

True progress—that is to say, moral progress—can occur only within the individual, and by his own effort.

But society is made up of people who can think only communally, in bands. Hence the "Belgian Schools".

There are also people who can entertain themselves only in a herd. The true hero finds his entertainment by himself.

XVI

The eternal superiority of the Dandy.

What is a Dandy?

XVII

My views on the theatre. What I have always liked best in a theatre, from my childhood to the present time, is the *chandelier*—a beautiful object, luminous, crystalline, complicated, circular and symmetrical.

Nevertheless I do not absolutely deny any merit to dramatic literature. Only I would like the actors to be raised on high buskins, wearing masks more expressive than the human face, and speaking through megaphones.

Lastly, I would like the women's rôles to be played by men.

After all, I've always thought that the chandelier was the principal actor—whether one regards it through the big end or the little end of one's opera-glass.

XVIII

One must work, if not from inclination, at least out of despair—since it proves, on close examination, that work is less boring than amusing oneself.

XIX

In every man, and at all times, there are two simultaneous yearnings—the one towards God, the other towards Satan.

The invocation of God, or spirituality, is a desire to ascend a step; the invocation of Satan, or animality, is a delight in descending. To this latter one should relate one's enamourments with women, one's intimate conversations with animals—dogs, cats etc. The pleasures derived from the two kinds of love correspond in nature to the loves themselves.

XX

Mankind's intoxication—a great picture to be painted:
in the style of charity;
in the style of libertinism;
in the literary, or actor's, style.

XXI

Questioning under torture is, as a means of discovering the truth, a barbaric stupidity; it is the employment of a material means to a spiritual end.

The death-penalty is the result of a mystical idea which nowadays is entirely misunderstood. The object of the death-penalty is not to "save" society—at least, not in the material sense—but to "save" (in the spiritual sense) both society and the culprit. So that the sacrifice may be perfect, there must be consent and joy on the part of the victim. To administer chloroform to a man condemned to death would be an impious act, for it would take from him the consciousness of his greatness as a victim, and would abolish his chance of gaining Paradise.

Dandies.

The reverse side of Claude Gueux. The theory of sacrifice. Legalisation of the death penalty. The sacrifice is made complete only by the *sponte sua* of the victim.

Imagine a man, condemned to death and then delivered from the executioner by the masses, thereupon voluntarily returning for execution. That would be a new justification for the death penalty.

As for torture, it has its origin in the infamous region of man's heart, the region that thirsts for sensual pleasures. Cruelty and sensual pleasure—identical sensations, like extreme heat and extreme cold.

XXII

My views on suffrage and the rights of the polling-booth. On the Rights of Man.

There is something base about any public function.

A Dandy does nothing. Can you imagine a Dandy speaking

to the people, unless to scoff at it?

The only reasonable and settled form of government is the aristocratic.

Monarchy and republic, when based on democracy, are equally absurd and weak.

Immense nausea of posters.

There are only three proper beings: the priest, the warrior, the poet. To know, to kill and to create.

All other men are malleable and subjugable, made to be put in harness—that is to say, to exercise what are called "professions".

XXIII

Worth noting that abolitionists of the death penalty must to a greater or less degree have an *interest* in its abolition.

Often they are guillotiners. The sum of it is: "I want to be able to cut your head off; but you shall not touch mine."

Abolitionists of souls ("materialists") are of necessity abolitionists of *Hell*. They, too, must certainly have an *interest* in the matter.

If nothing worse, they are people who are *afraid to live again*—lazy people.

XXIV

Madame de Metternich, although a princess, has forgotten to answer me concerning what I said about her and Wagner.

Nineteenth-century manners.

XXV

Story of my translation of Edgar Poe.

Story of *Fleurs du Mal*. Humiliation by misunderstanding, and my law-suit.

Story of my dealings with all the celebrities of the present time.

Fine sketches of a set of imbeciles:

Clément de Ris.

Castagnary.

Sketches of magistrates, functionaries, directors of magazines, etc.

Sketches of the artist in general.

Of the editor-in-chief, and of the whole world of governesses. Immense longing of the entire French people for governesses, for dictatorship. It is all simply: "If I were king!"

Sketches and anecdotes.

Francois Buloz—Houssaye—the famous Rouy—de Calonne—Charpentier, who amends the work of his authors, in virtue of the equality bestowed upon men by the immortal principles of 1789—Chevalier, a true editor-in-chief, Empire style.

XXVI

On George Sand.—That woman is the Prudhomme of immorality.

She has always been a moralist.

Only there was a time when her conduct was anti-moral.

Besides, she was never an artist. She has the famous "flowing style", dear to the bourgeoisie.

She is stupid, heavy and garrulous. Her ideas on morals have the same depth of judgment and delicacy of feeling as those of janitresses and kept women.

What she says about her mother.

What she says about poetry.

Her love of the working-class.

The fact that there are men who could become enamoured of this slut is indeed a proof of the abasement of the men of this generation.

Compare the preface to *Mademoiselle La Quintinie*, where she claims that true Christians do not believe in Hell.

La Sand speaks for *the God of the respectable*, the God of janitresses and knavish lackeys.

She has good reasons to wish to abolish Hell.

XXVII

The Devil and George Sand.—It must not be supposed that the Devil tempts only men of genius. He doubtless despises imbeciles, but he does not disdain their support. Quite on the contrary, he founds his greatest hopes upon such people.

George Sand, for example. She is, above all else, a *ponderous* animal; but also she is *possessed*. It was the Devil who persuaded her to rely on her "good heart" and her "good sense", so that she might persuade all the other ponderous animals to rely upon *their* good heart and good sense.

I cannot think of this stupid creature without a sort of shudder of repulsion. If I met her, I would be unable to refrain from throwing a stoup of holy-water at her head.

XXVIII

George Sand is one of those old leading-ladies of the stage who never want to quit the boards. I have recently been reading a preface by her—the preface to *Mademoiselle La Quintinie*—in which she claims that a true Christian does not believe in Hell. She has good reasons to wish to abolish Hell.

XXIX

I grow bored in France—and the main reason is that everybody here resembles Voltaire.

When Emerson wrote his *Representatives of Humanity*, he forgot Voltaire. He could have written an attractive chapter entitled: "Voltaire, or the anti-poet"—the king of nincompoops, the prince of the superficial, the anti-artist, the spokesman of janitresses, the Father Gigogne of the editors of *Siècle*.

XXX

In his *Lord Chesterfield's Ears*, Voltaire pokes fun at that immortal soul who for nine months dwelt amidst excrement and urine. Like all idlers, Voltaire hated mystery. He might at least have detected, in this choice of dwelling-place, a grudge or satire directed by Providence against love—and thus, in the method of procreation, a sign of Original Sin. After all, we can make love only with the organs of excretion.

Being unable to abolish love, the Church sought at least to disinfect it, and thus created marriage.

XXXI

Portrait taken from the underworld of letters.

Doctor Estaminetus Crapulosus Pedantissimus. His portrait done in the style of Praxiteles.

His pipe.

His opinions.

His Hegelianism.

His greasy squalor.

His ideas about art.

His rancour.

His envy.

A pretty picture of the younger generation.

XXXII

Φαρμακοτρίβης ἀνηρ καί τῶν τούς ὄφεις ἐς τὰ δώματα τρεφόντων—ELIEN

("Drug-pedlar, a man, and one of those who turn serpents into rods.")

XXXIII

Theology.

What is the Fall?

It is unity become duality, it is God who has fallen.

In other words, cannot the Creation be interpreted as the Fall of God?

Dandyism.—What is the superior man?

One who is not a specialist.

The man of leisure and broad Education.

The rich man who loves work.

XXXIV

Why does the man of intelligence prefer courtesans to society women—although both types are equally stupid? Find the answer.

XXXV

There are certain women who resemble the ribbon of the Legion of Honour. One has ceased to want them, because they have dirtied themselves on certain men.

For the same reason, I would not put on the trousers of a man who suffers from the itch.

The boring thing about love-making is that it's a crime for which one cannot dispense with an accomplice.

XXXVI

Research into that serious disease, hatred of the home. Pathology of the disease. Progressive growth of the disease.

Indignation caused by the universal fatuity of all classes, of all beings—of both sexes and of all ages.

Man loves his kind so much that, when he flees from the city, he does so in pursuit of the mob—that is to say, to reconstruct the city in the countryside.

XXXVII

Durandeau's views on the Japanese. ("For my part, I am first and foremost a Frenchman.")

"The Japanese are apes": I learnt this from no other than Darjon.

The views of that doctor who's a friend of Mathieu's, on the art of not having children, on Moses, and on the immortality of the soul.

"Art is an agent of civilisation."—Castagnary.

XXXVIII

Study of the facial expression of a sage and his family, on the fifth storey, drinking coffee.

Mr. Nacquart senior and Mr. Nacquart junior.

How Nacquart junior became a judge of the Court of Appeal.

XXXIX

On the Frenchman's passionate predilection for military metaphors. In this country every metaphor wears a moustache.

"The militant school of literature."
"Holding the fort."
"Carrying the flag high."
"Holding the flag high and secure."
"Hurling oneself into the thick of the fight."
"One of the Old Guard."
All these resounding expressions are applied, as a rule, to tavern pedants and idlers.

XL

French metaphors:
"Soldier of the judiciary press" (Bertin).
"The press militant."

XLI

More military metaphors:
"The poets of combat."
"The vanguard of literature."
This weakness for military metaphors is a sign of natures that are not themselves militant, but are made for discipline —that is to say, for conformity—natures congenitally domestic, Belgian natures that can think only in unison.

XLII

The love of pleasure binds us to the present. A care for our salvation links us to the future.
He who binds himself to pleasure—that is, to the present— seems to me like a man rolling down a slope, trying to cling to bushes, and uprooting them and carrying them with him in his fall.

The main thing is to be a "great man" and a "saint" *to oneself*.

XLIII

The masses' hatred of beauty. Examples: Jeanne and Mrs. Muller.

XLIV

Politics: The gist of it all, in the eyes of history and of the French people, is that Napoleon III's great claim to renown will have been that he showed how anybody at all, if only he gets hold of the telegraph and the printing-presses, can govern a great nation.

Those people are imbeciles who believe that such things can be done without the people's permission—and so are those who believe that fame can be founded only on virtue!

Dictators are the people's domestics—nothing more, and a damnable rôle, by the way—and fame is the result of the matching of a personality with the national stupidity.

XLV

What is love?
The need to escape from oneself.
Man is a worshipping animal.
To worship is to sacrifice oneself and to prostitute oneself.
Therefore all love is prostitution.

XLVI

The most prostituted being of all is the ultimate being—that is, God—since he is the supreme lover to each individual; since he is the communal, inexhaustible reservoir of love.

PRAYER

Do not punish me in the person of my mother, and do not punish my mother because of me. Guard the souls of my father and of Mariette. Give me the strength to do my duty promptly every day, and thus to become a hero and a saint.

XLVII

A chapter on the indestructible, eternal, universal and ingenious ferocity of mankind.

On blood-lust.

On intoxication with bloodshed.

On the intoxication of mobs.

On the intoxication of a person under torture (Damiens).

XLVIII

The only great ones of mankind are the poet, the priest and the soldier.

The man who sings, the man who sacrifices, and the man who sacrifices himself.

The rest are born to be whipped.

Have no trust in the people—or in good sense, good-heartedness, inspiration or evidence.

XLIX

I have always been amazed that women are allowed to enter churches. What sort of conversations can *they* have with God?

Eternal Venus (caprice, hysteria, fantasy) is one of the seductive manifestations of the Devil.

On the day when a young author corrects his first proof, he's as proud as a schoolboy who has just caught his first pox.

Mem. A long chapter on the art of divination by water, by cards, by reading hands, etc.

L

Woman cannot distinguish between soul and body. She is a simplifier, like the animals. . . A satirist would say that this is because she has nothing except a body.

A chapter on *The Dressing-Table*.

The moral significance of the dressing-table, and its pleasures.

LI

On pedantry,
on professors,
on judges,
on priests,
and on ministers.
The fine great men of today:
Renan.
Feydeau.
Octave Feuillet.
Scholl.
Directors of newspapers, Francois Buloz, Houssaye, Rouy, Girardin, Texier, de Calonne, Solar, Turgan, Dalloz.
A list of guttersnipes, with Solar at the top of the class.

LII

To be a great man and a saint *to oneself*, that's the only important thing.

LIII

Nadar is the most amazing expression of vitality. Adrien used to tell me that his brother Felix had all his vital organs in duplicate. I have felt envious at seeing him so successful in all matters not concerned with the abstract.

Veuillot is such a vulgarian and such an enemy of the arts that one might suppose that all the democracy in the world had taken refuge in his bosom.

Further development of the sketch:—supremacy of the pure idea amongst Christians and Babu-Communists alike.

A fantastical extreme of humility: not even to aspire to understand religion.

LIV

Music.
On slavery.
On society women.
On tarts.
On magistrates.
On the sacraments.
The man of letters is the world's enemy.
On bureaucrats.

LV

In love, as in almost all human affairs, sympathy is the result of a misunderstanding. This misunderstanding is the physical pleasure. The man cries out: "My angel!" The woman coos: "Mamma, mamma!" And the two imbeciles are convinced that they are thinking in harmony. The unbridgeable gulf which prevents communication remains unbridged.

G

LVI

Why is the sight of the sea so infinitely and eternally attractive?

Because the sea simultaneously provides the idea of immensity and of movement. To mankind six or seven leagues represent the radius of the infinite. A diminutive infinite, certainly—but what matter, if it suffices to suggest the idea of total infinity? Twelve or fourteen leagues of moving liquid suffice to provide the noblest idea of beauty that is offered to man in his transitory habitation.

LVII

The only interesting things on earth are the religions.

What is the universal religion (Chateaubriand, de Maistre, the Alexandrians, Capé)?

There is a universal religion, made for the alchemists of thought, a religion that emerges from man himself, man regarded as a divine memento.

LVIII

Evangelist Girardin has coined a phrase that will be remembered: *"Let us be mediocre!"*

Compare this with Robespierre's saying: "Those who do not believe in the immortality of their beings do themselves justice."

Evangelist Girardin's phrase implies an immense hatred of the sublime.

Anyone who has seen Evangelist Girardin walking in the street has been immediately struck by the notion of a big goose, deeply in love with herself, but scuttling over the road in panic to escape from a coach.

LIX

Theory of true civilisation. It does not consist in gas or steam or turn-tables. It consists in the diminution of the traces of Original Sin.

Peoples of nomads, shepherds, hunters, farmers and even cannibals can all be superior, by reason of their energy and personal dignity, to our Western races.

Perhaps these latter will be destroyed.

Theocracy and Communism.

LX

It is partly a life of leisure that has enabled me to increase my stature.

To my great detriment; for leisure, without fortune, accumulates debts and their resulting annoyances.

But to my great profit, as regards sensibility, meditation and the faculties of dandyism and dilettantism.

Other men of letters are, for the most part, base, ignorant swots.

LXI

The young lady beloved of editors.

The young lady beloved of editors-in-chief.

The young lady bugbear, monstrosity, assassin of art.

The young lady, what she really is:

A little fool and a little scoundrel; the greatest idiocy combined with the greatest depravity.

The young lady represents all the abject baseness of the street-urchin and the undergraduate.

LXII

Advice to non-Communists:

Everything is communal, even God.

G*

LXIII

The Frenchman is a farmyard animal, so well domesticated that he never dares to flutter over any fence. Compare his tastes in art and literature.

He's an animal of Latin race; he has no objection to ordure in his domicile, and in literature he is scatophagous. He delights in excrement. The scribblers of the tavern call it "Gallic salt".

A fine example of the baseness of France, of the people who claim to be more independent than those of any other nation. The following extract from M. de Vaulabelle's excellent book will suffice to give an idea of the impression made by Lavalette's escape upon the less enlightened portion of the Royalist party:

"At this moment of the second Restoration, royalist enthusiasm was carried, so to speak, to the point of mania. Young Joséphine de Lavalette was being educated at one of the principal Parisian convents, that of l'Abbaye-au-Bois; she left it only to go and embrace her father. When she returned to the convent after the escape, and when the very modest part she had played in it became known, an immense clamour was raised against the child. The nuns and her companions shunned her, and a good number of parents declared that they would withdraw their daughters from the convent if she were retained there. They did not wish, they said, to leave their daughters in contact with a young person who had indulged in such conduct and set such an example. Six weeks later, when Mrs. de Lavalette was set at liberty, she was obliged to remove her daughter from the convent."

LXIV

Princes and generations: It is equally unjust to attribute to reigning princes either the merits or the faults of the peoples whom they happen at a given moment to be governing.

These merits and faults are—as research and logic could show—almost always attributable to the atmosphere of the previous régime.

Louis XIV inherits men from Louis XIII: fame. Napoleon I inherits men from the Republic: fame. Louis-Philippe inherits men from Charles X: fame. Napoleon III inherits men from Louis-Philippe: disgrace.

It is always the previous regime that is responsible for the behaviour of its successor—in so far as a regime can be responsible for anything at all.

Abrupt terminations of reigns prevent this law from being absolutely exact in terms of time. One cannot exactly say when a given influence ceases; but it will certainly endure through the life of the generation that was exposed to it in youth.

LXV

On the hatred felt by young writers towards persons who quote excerpts from their work. To them the excerpter is an enemy.

"I would even make learning to write a capital offence." —Théophile Gautier.

Mem. a portrait of Fargues, the pirate and parasite of letters.

The human heart's ineradicable love of prostitution— source of man's horror of solitude. He wants to be *two*. The man of genius wants to be *one*—that is, solitary.

The glorious thing to do is to remain *one* by practising your prostitution in your own company.

This horror of solitude, this need to forget the "ego" in the flesh of another, is what men so nobly call "the need for love".

Two fine religions, everlastingly represented on the walls, the two eternal obsessions of the masses: on the one hand, the ancient phallus; and on the other hand "Hurrah for Barbès!" or "Down with Philippe!" or "Hurrah for the Republic!"

LXVI

Study, in all its manifestations, in the works of nature and the works of man, the universal and eternal law of growth by degrees, of "little by little" or "one thing at a time"— a growth accompanied by a steadily quickening accumulation of strength, like the accumulation of money at compound interest.

This applies also to *artistic and literary skill*, and also to that fluctuating treasure, *will-power*.

LXVII

The mob of minor authors whom one sees at funerals, distributing handshakes and impressing themselves upon the memories of reporters to the newspapers.

At the funerals of famous men.

LXVIII

Molière: My opinion of *Tartuffe* is that it is not a play, but a pamphlet. An atheist, merely if he is a man of good breeding, will be inspired by this piece to reflect that there are certain grave questions that should not be discussed in the presence of the masses.

LXIX

Praise the cult of images (my great, my unique, my primitive passion).

Praise vagabondage and what may be called "Bohemianism". Cult of sensation multiplied and expressed in music. Compare Liszt.

On the necessity that women should be beaten.

One can chastise what one loves—children, for example. But this entails the grief of despising what one loves.

On cuckoldry and cuckolds.

The grief of the cuckold.

It arises from his pride, from a false reasoning concerning honour and happiness, and from a love that has been foolishly diverted from God to be given to his creatures.

It is simply the worshipping animal disappointed in its idol.

LXX

A study in insolent imbecility. Clement de Ris and Paul Perignon.

LXXI

The more a man cultivates the arts, the less often he gets an erection.

He creates a more and more perceptible divorce between the spirit and the brute.

Only the brute gets really good erections, and copulation is the lyricism of the masses.

To copulate is to aspire to enter into another—and the artist never emerges from himself.

I've forgotten that slut's name. . . Oh, well, I'll be reminded of it on the Day of Judgment.

Music conveys the idea of space.

All the arts do this, more or less; for they employ *number*, and number is an interpretation of space.

Desire every day to be the greatest of men !

LXXII

As a child I sometimes wanted to be a Pope—but a military Pope—and sometimes to be an actor.

Delights that I had from these two daydreams.

LXXIII

While still quite a small child, I had in my heart two opposite feelings: a horror of life, and an ecstatic joy in life. Just the makings of a neurotic idler.

LXXIV

Nations have great men only despite themselves.

Apropos of the actor and the dreams of my childhood, a chapter on what creates in the human heart the actor's vocation; also on the actor's fame, his art and his place in society.

Legouvé's theory. Was Legouvé really a cold-blooded joker, a Swift who tried to see whether France could swallow a new absurdity?

His choice was a good one. Samson was not an actor.

On the true greatness of pariahs.

It may even be that virtue is jealous of the pariah's gifts.

LXXV

Commerce is essentially *satanic*. Commerce is a tit-for-tat, a loan given with the implication: "Give me back more than I give you".

The soul of every man of commerce is completely vitiated. Commerce is "natural", therefore *infamous*.

The least infamous of commercial people is the man who says: "Let me be virtuous, so as to earn much more money than the fools who are vicious."

For the commercial man, even honesty is a speculation for lucre.

Commerce is satanic because it is one of the forms of egoism, and the lowest and vilest.

LXXVI

When Jesus Christ said:
"Blessed are they that hunger, for they shall be fed," Jesus Christ was merely expressing a mathematical probability.

LXXVII

Society functions only by means of a misunderstanding.

A universal misunderstanding is what enables all society to function harmoniously.

For if, by some mischance, people understood each other, they would never be able to reach agreement.

The man of intelligence—he who will never agree with anybody—should study to acquire a love of the conversation of imbeciles, and a love of ill-written books. From these he will obtain bitter delights that will very largely compensate for his fatigue.

LXXVIII

Functionaries of any sort, ministers, managers of theatres or editors of newspapers, can now and then be estimable persons; but they can never be divine. They are persons without personality, beings without originality, born for their function—that is to say, for public domesticity.

LXXIX

God and his profundity: One can be not without intelligence and at the same time seek in God the counseller and friend who is always lacking. God is the eternal confidant, in that tragedy of which each of us is the hero. There are, perhaps, usurers and murderers who say to God: "Lord, grant that my next operation may be successful." But the prayers of these wretched people cannot spoil the honour and pleasure of my prayer.

LXXX

Every idea is of itself endowed with an immortal life, just as a person is. Every form created, even by man, is immortal. For form is independent of matter—form is not made up of molecules.

Bring in stories of Emile Douay and Constantin Guys destroying—or, rather, *supposing* that they were destroying —specimens of their work.

LXXXI

It is impossible to scan any periodical, of whatever day, month or year, without finding in every line of it evidence of the most appalling human perversity, together with the most surprising boasts of probity, goodness and charity and the most shameless assertions concerning progress and civilisation.

Every newspaper, from first line to last, is a tissue of horrors. Wars, crimes, thefts, acts of indecency, tortures, crimes by princes, crimes by nations, crimes by individuals, a debauch of universal villainy.

And this is the disgusting apéritif that the civilised man takes with his breakfast every morning. Everything in this world sweats with crime: the newspaper, the walls and men's faces.

I do not understand how any clean hand can touch a newspaper without a wince of disgust.

LXXXII

The power of the amulet, as demonstrated by philosophy: old coins with holes bored through them, talismans, everybody's memories.

A treatise on moral dynamic. On the virtue of the sacraments.

My tendency to mysticism, since my childhood. My conversations with God.

LXXXIII

On Obsession, Possession, Prayer and Faith.

The moral dynamic of Jesus.

Renan finds it ridiculous that Jesus should believe in the all-powerfulness, even in material matters, of Prayer and Faith.

The sacraments are instruments of this dynamic.

On the baseness of the printing-press—a great obstacle to the development of Beauty.

On organising a magnificent conspiracy to exterminate the Jewish race.

The Jews of the "Bibliothécaires" and witnesses of the "Redemption."

LXXXIV

All the imbeciles of the Bourgeoisie who interminably use the words: "immoral", "immorality", "morality in art" and other such stupid expressions remind me of Louise Villedieu, a five-franc whore who once went with me to the Louvre. She had never been there before, and began to blush and cover her face with her hands, repeatedly plucking at my sleeve and asking me, as we stood before deathless statues and pictures, how such indecencies could be flaunted in public.

The fig-leaves of Mr. Nieuwerkerke.

LXXXV

In order that there should be a law of progress, everybody would have to desire to create it. In other words, humanity will progress just as soon as individuals study how to do so.

This argument may serve to explain the identity of the two opposed ideas of freedom and of predestination. . . Not only will progress entail the identity of these two—this identity has always existed. This identity is history—the history of nations and of individuals.

LXXXVI

A sonnet worth quoting in *My heart laid bare*. Remember to quote also the piece on Roland.

Phyllis, I dreamed this night, within my chamber showed
As lovely as erstwhile beneath the light of day,
Seeking to give her ghost again to amorous play,
That, like Ixion, I should couple with a cloud.

Her ghost crept in my bed, naked, without a shroud,
And said: "Dear Damon, back to thee I find my way.
"I am but grown more fair whilst I did darkling stay
"In that grim region whence at last I am allowed.

"I come to kiss again the handsomest of blades,
"I come to die again within thy body's mesh."
Then, when the image had exacted its full toll,

It said: "Farewell! And now I go back to the shades.
"Since thou hast boasted oft of lying with my flesh,
"Now canst thou boast anew, of lying with my soul."
                            —*The satirical Parnassus.*

I think this sonnet is by Maynard. Malassis asserts that it's by Théophile.

LXXXVII

A regular life—plans: the more one desires, the better one desires.

The more one works, the better one works, and the more one wishes to work.

The more one produces, the more fertile one becomes.

After a debauch one always feels more lonely, more forsaken.

In moral as in physical matters, I have always been aware of the abyss—not merely the abyss of sleep, but the abyss of action, memory, desire, regret, remorse, beauty, number, etc.

I cultivated my hysteria with delight and terror. Now I suffer from continual vertigo, and today, January 23rd, 1862, I had a signal warning:—I felt passing over me the wind of the wing of imbecility.

LXXXVIII

A regular life. Morals: Off to Honfleur! As soon as possible, before I sink lower.

How many presentiments and signs has God already sent me, that it is now *urgently* time to *take action*—to regard this present minute as the most important of all minutes, and to make a *perpetual enjoyment* of what is ordinarily my torment; that is to say, of Work!

LXXXIX

A regular life. Conduct. Morals: Every minute we are crushed by the idea and sense of time. There are only two methods of escaping from this nightmare, of forgetting it: physical pleasure, and work. Pleasure wears us out. Work strengthens us. Let us make our choice.

The more we resort to either one of these methods, the more we shrink from the other.

One can never forget time except when putting it to use.

Nothing can be done except little by little.

De Maistre and Edgar Poe taught me how to think.

No task is a long one but the task on which one dare not start. It becomes a nightmare.

XC

A regular life: By putting off what is to be done, one runs the risk of never being able to do it. By not seeking conversion immediately, one risks damnation.

As a remedy against all ills—poverty, sickness and melancholy—only one thing is absolutely necessary: *a liking for work.*

XCI

Valuable notes: Do every day what duty and prudence demand.

If you worked every day, your life would be more endurable. Work for *six* days without stopping.

As for finding subjects, *gnothi seauton*.

(List of things I like).

Always be a poet, even in prose.

The grand style (nothing is more beautiful than the commonplace).

First of all, get started, and after that apply logic and analysis. Any argument, no matter what, is worth following to its conclusion.

Discover day-to-day excitement.

XCII

A regular life. Conduct. Morals: Two parts. Debts (Ancelle). Friends (Mother, friends, myself).

Thus, every 1,000 francs to be divided into two parts of 500 each, and the second subdivided into three parts.

At Honfleur: Survey and classify all my letters (two days) and all my debts (two days). (Four categories—*notes of hand, big debts*, little debts, friends). Classify my engravings (two days). Classify my notes (two days).

XCIII

A regular life. Morals. Conduct: Too late, perhaps!— Mother and Jeanne.—Charity and duty demand that I regain health.—Jeanne's illnesses, Mother's infirmities and solitude.

—Do one's duty daily, and trust in God for the morrow. —The only way of earning money is to work disinterestedly.

—Short summary of good conduct: care of the person, prayer, work.

—Prayer: charity, goodness, strength.

—Without charity, I am nothing but a sounding cymbal.

—My humiliations have been God's blessings.

—Is my phase of egoism at an end?

—The faculty of responding to the need of each minute (of exactitude, in a word) must inevitably find its reward.

"Unhappiness, when prolonged, has on the soul the same effect as old age on the body: one can no longer be active; one goes to bed. . .

"On the other hand, extreme youth offers arguments for procrastination. When one has plenty of time in store, one persuades oneself that one can spend years in dalliance before events will overtake one."—*Chateaubriand*.

XCIV

A regular life. Conduct. Morals: Jeanne 300, Mother 200, myself 300—800 francs a month. Work from six o'clock in the morning, without eating, until noon. Work blindly, at random, like a lunatic. We'll see what comes of it.

I seem to be entrusting my whole destiny to working without interruption for several hours at a time.

Nothing is irreparable. There is still time. Who knows, even, whether new pleasures. . .?

Fame, payment of my debts—*wealth* for Jeanne and Mother.

I have never yet known the pleasure of carrying out a plan. Power of the preconceived idea, power of hope.

The habit of doing one's duty drives away fear.

I must wish to dream, and I must know how to dream. How to evoke inspiration. Magical art. Set about writing *at once*. I spend too much time in arguing with myself.

Work done immediately, even if ill done, is better than daydreaming.

A series of small acts of will add up to a great total.

Every shrinking from the exercise of the will is the loss of a particle of substance. How prodigal, therefore, is hesitation! And imagine the immensity of the effort finally necessary to repair so much loss!

The man who says his prayers in the evening is a captain posting his sentries. After that, he can sleep.

Dreams about death, warning portents.

Hitherto I have always enjoyed my memories alone: I must enjoy them in another's company. Make a passion of the joys of the heart.

Because I can conceive of a glorious existence, I believe that I can achieve it. Ah, Jean-Jacques!

Work necessarily begets wholesome habits, sobriety and chastity—and consequently health, wealth, a successive and progressive creative genius, and, lastly, charity. *Age quod agis*.

Fish, cold baths, showers, Iceland moss, sweetmeats occasionally; in any case, complete abstinence from all stimulants.

Iceland moss . . . . 4½ oz.
White sugar . . . . 9 oz.

Soak the moss for 12–15 hours in a sufficient quantity of cold water; then strain the water off. Boil the moss in a half-gallon of water, over a slow, steady flame, until the half-gallon has been reduced to a quart; then skim once. Now add the 9 oz. of sugar, and let the mixture thicken to the consistency of a syrup. Leave standing until cold. Take *three* large spoonfuls daily, every morning, noon and evening. In the event of very frequent attacks, do not hesitate to increase the dose.

XCV

A regular life. Conduct. Method: I solemnly promise myself that I shall henceforth adopt the following as the guiding rules of my life.

Say my prayers every morning to God, *reservoir of all strength and all justice,* invoking *my father, Mariette and Poe* as intercessors for me. Pray to all these to communicate to me *the necessary strength* for the discharge of all my duties, and to grant that my mother may *live long enough* to rejoice in my transformation. Work all day long, or, at least, *to the limits of my powers.* Trust in God—that is to say, in Justice itself—that my projects will be successful. Say every evening a new prayer, asking God for life and strength for my mother and myself. Divide all I earn into four parts—one for day-to-day expenses, one for my creditors, one for my friends, and one for my mother. Adhere to principles of the strictest sobriety; the first of which is complete abstinence from all stimulants of any kind.

III

YEARS IN BRUSSELS

I

I have spent fifteen years in the company of the maniacal, the extravagant, the half-mad; and for this reason I myself have been taken for a sort of better-dressed Watripon. Nevertheless, these fifteen years were not entirely wasted: they procured for me a few accurate ideas concerning the necessity of leading an intensely moral life: an exemplary life—lived, so to speak, in front of a mirror.

II

"The Devil turns hermit." To taunt a person with these words is to blame him for not continuing to lead a despicable existence. It is strange to see how the populace confuses perseverance (which it rightly regards as a virtue of the first order) with obstinacy.

III

Rue de Mercélis, Ixelles.—Lacroix, Verboeckhoven, 2, rue Royale.—Elise, imp. du Courbet.

IV

Only artists and children have the gift of vividly appreciating images. For these privileged beings, an image represents *something else:* a dream that they recall, a miraculous voyage, a minute of salvation. This appreciation, by the way, has nothing in common with the "appreciation" of certain art-lovers who merely collect agreeable chattels. The "appreciation" of the collector is vitiated by too great variety, or by other influences. The child and the artist continually discover new themes in a single image; and their appreciation is variegated by the manner in which the charm of an image shifts and presents itself to them in new forms.

V

Horton's, Villa-Hermosa, Montagne de la Cour.—The Union Tavern, rue N.—D. aux neiges.—Le Globe, 5, place Royale.—Hymans, chaussée de Vleurgat.

VI

In this country they celebrate the festivals of Bacchus by drinking "faro".* Belgian drunkenness is a series of hiccups. When a Belgian is drunk, he thinks he is behaving like a drunkard; but in fact he is merely behaving like a Belgian.

Moreover, there are two kinds of drunkenness: the church-goers' kind and the free-thinkers' kind. Both kinds are garrulous, and pick their arguments out of the gutter.

The country of indecent assaults. Exhibitionism. Bestiality, scatology, the "little man" at his worst.

Just as Burgundy is the wine country, so Brussels is the "faro" country—in other words, the country of urine.

VII

What a woman chiefly asks of her male accomplice is that

* A Belgian beer.

he should be virile. What she asks of God is that he should
be omnipotent.

I have several times written that woman is the opposite
of the aristocrat. She never does violence to her own nature:
which means that sinning comes as naturally to her as eating
or drinking. Besides, she has no notion of how to control
herself.

Woman sees in God a superior type of man—a combination
of all other men, the peerless embracer: all the more potent
because he is more huge. Inescapably, there is something
unclean about woman's religious credo, and about the
outpourings of this credo.

The demon, imagination and women.

The strange thing about woman—her preordained fate—
is that she is *simultaneously* the sin and the Hell that
punishes it.

VIII

Josse Sacré, 10, Canfersteen.—A. Bluff, 49, rue du Midi.—
Kiessling, 26, Montagne de la Cour.—Rosez, 87, rue
Madeleine.—Olivier, 5 bis, rue des Paroissiens.

IX

Against a black sky, figures as geometrical as crystals of
snow—in two dimensions. Then the sky's silk is crumpled
from behind, as if birds' claws were plucking at it in a
regular pattern. The crystals grow brighter, phosphorescent.
And the whole scene blossoms into a great prism with a
thousand facets: *the chandelier*.

X

Vulgarity of Belgian jokes.

Belgian names have a vulgarly joking sound—splendid

material for the gentlemen who write farces for the music-halls: Sacré, Josse, Vandenpereboom.

XI

Business is simply a nexus of infamous intrigues. So-called "respectable" business-men are fully aware of this. Hence their systematic reserve and politeness. They realise their guilt.

The customer, too, can make his purchases in a spirit of lust for lucre (collectors, speculators); but, even so, his activities will never be so essentially satanic as those of the merchant. Profit, rate of interest, so-much-per-cent: those are the things that indicate the difference.

The Belgian business-man, in all that he does, is guilty of forcing the note. When he wishes to be agreeable, he is familiar; when he wishes to be polite, he is obsequious. The vulgar caricatured by the trivial.

XII

Dictionary of metaphors: A woman whose marriage makes her an accessory before the crime.

The tirades in *Justine* have furnished extensive material for journalists.

XIII

Wiertz, the great painter of these parts. Painting in the style of the Encyclopaedists, philosophical and humanitarian pretentions, belief in Progress. Appalling specimen of stupidity and rascality.

XIV

How many people can one number whose minds are ready to admit that audacity in matters of art is not necessarily disingenuous? A new thing is thought excusable—and is, in fact, excused—only if people can find in it clearly-marked signs of its ancestry. The journalists reproach Manet with producing pastiches of Goya—just as they used to compare Petrus Borel to de Sade.

XV

The exploitation of journalism. Journalism and business. Here's an advertisement (of English origin) that sounds a fairly grotesque note. Its object is to sell Indians little statues of their gods:

"Yamen, god of day, cast in pure copper and tastefully worked; Nirondi, prince of demons, in great variety. The giant upon whom he rides is boldly designed, and his sword is fashioned in the most modern style. Baronnin, god of the sun, very lifelike; his crocodile is of copper, with a silver tail. Bouberen, god of wealth: this god is entirely choice, of the finest workmanship (*sic*), and the manufacturers have taken the greatest pains to achieve a perfect likeness. Small demi-gods, and other lower deities, in the greatest variety. No credit is given, but there is a discount on cash payments."

XVI

Heusner, 16, place Sainte-Gudule.—Van Trigt, 30, rue Saint-Jean.—Claassen, 88, rue Madeleine.

XVII

Women: suety complexions; tow hair; enormous throats and stomachs; fat, red hands; swollen ankles. Faces strongly marked with idiocy. The detritus of a race—just as there *are* stupid negroes.

With them, fornication must have a remarkable resemblance to a mere task, and a very squalid one. All notion of pleasure is made impossible.

Absence of conditions necessary for physical pleasure. Frequency of rapes committed in the evenings, when customers are leaving the taverns. A people conceived in drunkenness and excrement.

XVIII

In France a political campaign, of whatever sort, is looked on as a disgusting affair.

In Belgium, where charlatanism is the rule, the voter is (or pretends to be) a serious person, convinced of the sincerity with which he votes.

Reasoning of a Belgian voter:

1. "I am anti-clerical, I read Mr. Hugo's books and I vote for the triumph of Truth (progress, justice, jobbery, etc.)". . . Worth noting in passing that this voter is the father of a family, and sleeps with his eldest daughter; also that he's a restaurant proprietor by trade, and sells his customers rotten conserves.

2. "My neighbour, also a voter, is far from possessing my intelligence or my knowledge of affairs. He's going to vote all wrong. Let us go and explain his duty to him."

The Belgian Chamber, stupidity raised to the power of three.

The Latin American republics, always seething, always in a state of insurrection, are perhaps the only institutions with which one can feel some sympathy. The point is that there is always something fantastic in their violence.

After all, down there people kill each other over such matters.

The Belgians tread on each other's toes and abuse each other in Flemish.

XIX

Ph. Delacre, 86, Montagne de la Cour.

XX

What romances of the seventeenth century used to call "the lightning-stroke", deciding the destiny of the hero and his beloved, is a movement of the soul which—although it has been spoilt by an infinite number of hacks—nevertheless does exist in nature; it arises from the impossibility of any defensive manoeuvre. A woman who loves is too happy in her feelings to be able successfully to dissemble them. Tired of prudence, she neglects all precaution and blindly gives herself up to the happiness of loving. Distrust, on the other hand, precludes all possibility of the "lightning-stroke".

The "lightning-stroke" is mental laziness. The woman is in a hurry to surrender because she supposes that, from a certain moment onwards, it is impossible for her to defend herself. She wants to be ———, and this noble desire costs her any powers of judgment she may have had. The man is delighted, and hastens to discover moral qualities in his accomplice. She, meanwhile, appreciates her lover's virility. Each of them thinks of his or her own personal happiness. The "lightning-stroke" is a mistake which lovers lack either the courage or the discernment to recognise as they commit it.

A matter in which God has shown an infinite cunning is in contriving two creatures so deeply strange to one another that every step they take in their mutual dealings may be a false one. To be a saint is to parody God's clear-sightedness.

There is charity in a man's love for a stupid woman, just as there is paederasty in the same man's love for an intelligent woman.

XXI

Awoken by his excitement, he turned his face to the wall, shut his eyes and was so fortunate as to catch hold of his dream just as it slipped over the bedside.

XXII

The absurd thing about a religion of progress is that it tends to substitute, in place of a hierarchy, a class-system based entirely on practical utility.

The vulgar preferred to the refined, the banal to the precious, the short-story to the poem, etc. The strict development of such a system ends in the idiot's prevailing over the madman, and an infinity of anomalies of the same sort.

Demand for the abolition of the death-penalty—its object, clearly, that assassins interested in such a measure may not be interrupted in their "utilitarian" tasks.

XXIII

"Mrs. ——— disposes of a large selection of wealthy young ladies and widows seeking matrimony."

Prostitution, bourgeois style. To marry instead of going to the brothel, to plight troth instead of paying.

XXIV

On the pompous style of Belgian polemics.

The mutual suspicion of the Bruxellois. "Spies" at the windows. Police-States, States of supervision.

XXV

An unexpected consequence of this much-talked-of "progress" will be that gambling will become respectable. The laws of chance are certainly no less valid than those of newspaper directors. One can choose between the sub-editors' room and the gaming hell.

The press, feeding on crimes of every sort.

There are gamblers who are equally fond of winning and of losing.

This new cult of progress, beloved of idlers and scoundrels, will prove to have been the main characteristic of our time. Stupidity doing homage to itself, steam-engines denying God.

On the necessity for superstitions:

The most vulgar sort of superstition—superstitions concerning water, flame, nature, revolving tables—would have been preferable to the superstition of progress, based solely on vanity.

The negro is superstitious about the moon; the horse about the whip. Man has taken himself as his own idol.

Soon God will be elected by universal suffrage.

XXVI

Hérard: Death of Antonio Watripon?

Write to Ancelle—to Julien Lemer—to Jousset—to Villemessant.

Pauvre Belgique. Spleen de Paris and my *Fleurs.*

XXVII

Malines, country of tranquillity.

This spot is a refuge for those two dozen Belgians who

have reached years of discretion. Light sagaciously
distributed over a sleepy little town. Houses arranged round
the churches: Jesuit churches, in a somewhat pompous
style, full of curves and faceted rose-work.

Grass in the streets, music, carillons, running waters.

Jouvenet, Restout.

XXVIII

Legion of Honour given to Varin, Antier, Lambert
Thiboust.

That Cross is handed out like a penal sentence. It has its
judges and its delinquents.

XXIX

Greuse, 1, rue du Boulevard.

What Belgians dislike about Miss Boschetti's dancing is
that the dancer is "rather short." That's what their newspapers say.

Amina may aspire, flutter and soar and smile,
The Belgian says: "That sort of thing is not my style.
"The only woodland nymphs I've any wish to know
"Are those who live my way, down Kitchen-Garden Row."

From her fine-pointed shoe, and from her laughing eye,
Amina pours out floods of wit and ecstasy.
The Belgian says: "They're lies, they are not true to life,
"These flighty ways—they don't remind me of my wife."

Little you know, O sylph, so proudly jubilant,
You who would teach the waltz unto the elephant,
Teach laughter to the stork, irony to the owl,

That blazing beauty makes the Belgian yelp with fear;
That if sweet Bacchus poured Burgundy in his bowl,
The monster would reply: "I'd rather have some beer!"

XXXI

The chief characteristic of the excremental authors is their lack of imagination. Sometimes it's their violence that rescues them from oblivion. Calumny: Bussy-Rabutin, Blessebois. — Delirium: Sade. — Voluptuaries: Cleland, Narciat.—Restif de la Bretonne.

XXXII

Father Hermann, mixture of strength and subtlety. One of the "means" by which God wins us.

(One-time accompanist to Liszt, Father Superior of the Carmelite monastery in London).

XXXIII

In his inability to know whether his acts conform to God's will, man's best course is to observe the strictest rules of morality.

The difficulty of continually doing what is admirable exemplifies the difficulty of *continually* drawing nearer to God.

Make a point of triumphing over difficulties, so as to earn double wages: pleasure and salvation.

XXXIV

According to free-thinkers' logic, Christians are, without exception, persons of bad faith and devotees of an absurd superstition.

There is no valid argument against the existence of God, because the primary basis of any such argument must be contained within the foregoing statement.

Excuse for Malassis:

"The Divine Will is incomprehensible to me, and my mind is barred from it by doubt and anguish. My anguish, therefore, is irreducible. So let me live for the day."

XXXV

Strange as it may seem, the Belgians regard "refinement" as a prime virtue in art and literature. That is why they are so fond of Wiertz, Verbeckhoven, George Sand or the younger Dumas; and it is in the name of this last that Frédéric attacks Ponson du Terrail.

A disciple of Béranger, a Belgian Béranger: Bovie.

Lemercier de Neuville's *pupazzi* have begun to talk Belgian—thanks to Mr. Flor O'Squarr, author of *Ouye! Ouye! Ouye!*

Brussels, country of apes. Counterfeits of courtesans and whores.

Malassis saying to Nadar, when the latter had suffered from certain Belgian rascalities: "One does not roll in the mire with impunity."

XXXVI

Outre-Quiévrain. *Make him ridiculous.*

XXXVII

They think that evil has a stunting effect. Quite on the contrary, evil is capable—not, indeed, of uplifting one—but *perhaps* of adding to one's stature.

XXXVIII

Brussels, cigar and cigarette vendors.

Every big street has some lingering trace of the old festivals—a depressing trace.

Place de l'Hôtel-de-Ville: The style of Louis XIV has become what everything becomes here. Apotheosis of merchandising. Monument to commerce.

Franklinisation before its time.

XXXIX

November 10th, 1864: Until I receive *proof* that in the real struggle (that against time) I am bound to be defeated, I shall not permit myself to say that I have made a failure of my life. All the same. . . .

XL

Morality: A singular consequence of the present development of the press is that principles which in former times were declared from the height of the pulpit, with the authority of priesthood, are today proclaimed and defended by the honourable corporation of professional journalists— amongst whom there is today not a single man left who isn't a police-spy. Touching legion of archangels!

XLI

What the best draughtsmen of our time (and perhaps those of future times will do the same) specially seize upon to caricature in order to create a sense of our epoch, are particular aspects of the ridiculous.

In former times (up to the eighteenth century) they selected aspects of the sublime.

Here everybody talks at the top of his voice. But the main characteristic of the city (if one disregards the whistles and barkings) is its silence.

Paris, which is a city full of noises, perhaps lives upon them.

XLII

Met yesterday a certain rather doubtful and queer personage, who gave me much food for thought. A personage much concerned with various forms of mischief.

"There is only one thing that really brings misfortune," he said: "our custom of offering good wishes for the New Year. Nobody knows this, and that is why humanity is so misfortunate. . . "

XLIII

Romanticism: When we ponder on the days of our youth, we think of them as a manifestation of ourselves. We are, in fact, resurrecting ourselves—and, around us, an epoch.

Reconstructions of bygone ages are false in this respect, that there is no life at their centre—everything has the same depth: the result is inevitably a chromolithograph.

Prostitution is essentially a matter of lack of choice. Yet the vocabulary and the aesthetic creed of prostitution always seek to give an impression that choice is somehow present.

What is it that makes a masterpiece? Dürer.

I like to imagine an art in which the quality of lastingness would be replaced by that of the provisional. An art constantly *applied* to life. Theatres. Seasons. Sunshine. Dancers and dancing.

XLIV

Brussels Free University and public instruction.

To combat ignorance is to diminish God.

The drunken dream of the humanitarian—abolition of the death-penalty.

Believing themselves to have abolished sin, the free-thinkers thought it would be clever to put an end to courts of justice and abolish punishment. That's what they call, quite accurately, "progress."

Words of the younger Flourens:

"In the imagination of poets, humanity starts with a Golden Age, a state of happiness, from which it promptly falls. This same false notion is found in the myths of religion. Science, on the contrary, teaches us that at first peoples led an entirely animal existence, and that since then our species has been making a slow, often interrupted, but assured progress."

Weill and the younger Flourens, singing the drawing-room ditties of Free Thought.

XLV

Faure, Hôtel Royal, rue des Fossés-aux-Loups.

Belgian Societies:—The Philanthropic Friendly Society, the Adelphi Dramatic Society.

Bellini, marsala with cinchona and calumba root, chez Delacre.

THE SOHO BOOK COMPANY

**THE DEAD SEAGULL,
by GEORGE BARKER**
I warn you that as you lie in your
bed and feel the determination of
your lover slipping its blade
between your ribs, this is the real
consummation. "Kill me, Kill
me," you murmur. But it always
surprises you when you die.
ISBN 0948166 00 2 / £4.95

**THE ENCHANTED
WANDERER,
by NICOLAI LYESKOV**
He deserves the privilege of
standing with Tolstoy. (M. Gorky)
ISBN 0948166 04 5 / £5.95

**SELECTED LETTERS of
FRIEDRICH NIETZSCHE**
Visions have appeared on my
horizon the like of which I have
never seen.
ISBN 0948166 01 0 / £6.95

**MARIUS THE EPICUREAN,
by WALTER PATER**
The only great prose in modern
English. (W.B. Yeats)
ISBN 0948166 02 9 / £7.95

**ARMANCE,
by STENDHAL**
A neglected masterpiece. (A. Gide)
ISBN 0948166 03 7 / £5.95

**DOMINIQUE,
by EUGENE FROMENTIN**
I feel myself a child before a man
who has reflected so much.
(George Sand)
ISBN 0948166 06 1 / £4.95

**AXEL,
by VILLIERS de l'ISLE-
ADAM**
Admirable, but mad. (J.P. Sartre)
ISBN 0948166 053 / £4.95

1 BREWER STREET LONDON W1R 3FN TELEPHONE 01–439 0100